Prai

"Stark, moody. ... Sami cul-
ture and her po ... restigators
take the novel far beyond a genre ....ment."
—Sandra Scofield, *Newsday*

"Remarkable...More than a mere murder story, *Under the Snow* is a fine presentation of the tensions of life in an isolated village."
—Ken Wisneski, *Minneapolis Star Tribune*

"Haunting...intricate...Overweight, irascible Constable Torsson [is] Ekman's flintiest and finest creation."
—*Raleigh News and Observer*

"Superb...great literary style."
—*Progress Tribune* (Phoenix)

"Outstanding...taut and atmospheric...Ekman's skill at understated characterization is the quality that lifts her novels out of the genre and into universal resonance."
—*Publishers Weekly*

"Eerie...dazzling...Irresistible: Save this one for a wintry night by the fireside."
—*Kirkus Reviews*

"Brilliant...compelling...mysterious."
—*Library Journal*

Other books by Kerstin Ekman

available in English

BLACKWATER

KERSTIN

EKMAN

Translated from the

Swedish by Joan Tate

Picador USA

New York

UNDER THE SNOW

Picador® is a U.S. registered trademark and is used by St. Martin's Press under license from Pan Books Limited.

For information on Picador USA Reading Group Guides, as well as ordering, please contact the Trade Marketing department at St. Martin's Press.
Phone: 1-800-221-7945 extension 488
Fax: 212-677-7456
E-mail: trademarketing@stmartins.com

ISBN 0-312-20038-2

First published in Sweden as *De tre små mas mästerna* by Albert Bonniers Forlag.

First Published in English by Vintage, Random House UK.

First Picador USA Edition: February 1999

10 9 8 7 6 5 4 3 2 1

Contents

UNDER THE SNOW

1. RAKISJOKK'S UPPER TEN

He had been fighting with a fly all morning. Starving, it had overwintered between the venetian blind and the inner pane of the duty-room window. It was staggering around in there, occasionally tumbling head over heels—if it had heels. He was swiping at it with the ruler but couldn't reach to give it the coup de grâce.

His fingers grew numb with cold and he had to close

the window. His eyes having adjusted to darkness months ago, he thought he could make out the curved outline of the ore mountain out there in the dark. In fact, he knew it was there only from the glimmering lights of the road up to the mine. In the street below the window Fredriksson was walking back and forth on the second hour of his beat, his baton jiggling on its lead.

He picked up his pen and drew a large sun on the blotting paper. He had to put the pen down to keep from overdecorating the sun and ruining the blotter, which would have to last all March. He could not even raise a smile at the willpower that cost him.

Shortly afterward he worked out what to do about the fly. He loosened the cords of the blind and jerked the slats vigorously up and down. When he fastened the cords again, the fly had found peace. Meanwhile the telephone had emitted at least five rings. It could wait.

He lifted the receiver and at first heard nothing but crackling and buzzing. The call must come from somewhere outside the town, he realized. It had been snowing heavily for the last few days and the wires were down in several places up toward the mountain. Then he heard a voice—monkey chatter in the buzz—saying it was Vuori from Rakisjokk and could he hear him? Was that the police?

"Yes!" he yelled. "This is the police. Torsson speaking." Then the connection faded.

He sat staring at Fredriksson, who had now stopped under the streetlamp and was rubbing his face with his woolen mittens. Then he moved on, a large black patch in all that shadowy white. The streetlights were dancing in the wind and casting patches of light that made everything appear to be moving in the stillness.

"Matti Olsson's dead. Matti at the school."

He started at the sudden voice stabbing his ear.

"You'll have to come on up here. He's been struck down."

The words reached him as a murmur of rising and falling waves.

"Who did it?" Torsson yelled.

"Seems to be Erik Sjögren."

"The man who does the measurements?"

"Aye, taking care of the weather for us. You'd better come on up here. We can't talk like this. Can't hear properly."

Well, that was news. Torsson felt like hurling the telephone through the window.

"What's he doing now, then? He hasn't gone up the mountain, has he?"

"No, he's still here."

"How are we supposed to get up there?" Torsson asked, then added, with the singular foolishness that occasionally surprised even himself, "The lake's frozen over."

"You'll have to ski from Orjas."

"That's twenty-five kilometers!" Torsson yelled, but the other man seemed not to hear. "Are you sure it'll bear?"

Had he heard the other man laughing? Or was it just malicious wind spirits swinging to and fro on the wires?

"We'll phone back," said Torsson, "and tell you when we can be at Orjas."

But the caller didn't want to hear that. "I'll leave straight away," he said. "See you early tomorrow morning in Orjas. I'll stay the night at Anna's."

"But we've got to get over to you tonight," Torsson shouted. "We need to hear what's happened."

"We can't cross the lake tonight anyhow, and I haven't got much to tell you."

"How did it happen?"

But by then the connection had already been cut. Torsson sat with the receiver in his hand, staring at the silent little holes in the Bakelite. Had the other man hung up or the wires come down, or had the infernal weather up here blown away the whole of Rakisjokk? Anyway, it was silent. He finally replaced the receiver and sat staring at the sun on his blotter.

Just like Torsson, the chief of police of this mining town had originally come from the south. Having carried out his duties for thirty-five years among a taciturn breed in a country where the winter is five thousand and sixty-four hours long, he had lost some of the animation in his speech and the cheerfulness that he associated with brightly lit shopping streets and apple blossom. He did not like to be disturbed. When Torsson turned up to give his report, he saw fit to wave the paper in his hand to make a show of the urgency and importance of his errand. He gave a halting account of what he'd heard over the phone.

"We're to meet at Orjas and he'll take us across the lake," he said, adding gloomily, "on skis, of course."

The police chief's gaze was lost in the dark rectangle of the window. He was breathing heavily and thinking about something else.

"Huh," he said suddenly. He swung around and looked at Torsson. "Killing each other, that they can manage. But as for building roads . . ."

Taking the inhabitants of Norrbotten all in all, as the police chief did, there was a certain—albeit not particularly amiable—logic in the statement.

"Early tomorrow morning, of course," said Torsson.

The police chief was studying the pools form in front of him, having apparently lost interest in the subject. Thoughtfully, he put down a cross and covered himself with a one. Torsson's boots creaked with as much impatience as he dared allow them.

"You'll just have to go then," his chief said abruptly. "Take Fredriksson with you."

"Me?" Annoyingly, his voice soared into falsetto and he noted a gray look over those spectacles.

"Torsson, aren't you fit and ready?" He moistened his aniline pen and covered himself with a two as well. "And you have skis?"

"Yes," said Torsson. "Of course."

He snatched back the paper from the desk, made a combined bow and half salute, and left.

Fredriksson received the message about the coming twenty-five-kilometer trip halfway through his cabbage soup. He took it with the calm of which only a native of north of the Arctic Circle and an ex-rifleman is capable.

They left in the dark morning with the cold creeping up on them. Bolin drove them in the police car the forty kilometers to Orjas, grinning at their rucksacks and anoraks and calling them fitness freaks. Fredriksson looked bright and cheery under his protective layer of ointment and said he hadn't been to Rakisjokk since the rifle corps had built an observation post by the glacier.

"And now, of course, you're simply dying to go back," said Torsson.

"Not exactly." said Fredriksson frankly, "but I suppose I have to. It comes with the job."

Forty kilometers and three quarters of an hour later,

however, he was in no state to follow the call of duty his rifleman's heart had felt. He was sitting on the shore of the Rakisjaure like a mysterious X in the snow, one ski broken and his ankle sprained, looking surprised more than anything else. Behind him was a recently churned fifty-meter track up to Anna Salminen's cottage in Orjas.

"You have to watch out for these sharp-edged lake shores," Vuori remarked, leaning over him. Henrik Vuori was around forty-five, a squat, sinewy man who owned a boat and ran the tourist trips on the Rakisjaure in the summer. He was considered a man to be reckoned with out here.

Fredriksson couldn't put any weight on his foot and Torsson had to hurry up to Anna's cottage. Anna's two sons were out driving loads, so she thrust her feet into ski straps and pulled the Sami sledge, which is like a lace-up kayak, behind her. In the summer she served coffee to the tourists by the pier, but at this time of year she was alone and open to fresh events.

"*Herra jumala* [My God], what a thing to happen!" she cried as she caught sight of Fredriksson in the snow. "Up on the sledge with you, man, and we'll see if anything's broken. Come on, you two. No, don't put your weight on it," she went on, meaning the foot in its double-laced army boot.

Once inside the warmth of her cottage, Fredriksson had to submit to Anna unlacing his boot and pulling off all three pairs of socks until his foot lay exposed and pale like forced rhubarb on the reindeer skin covering the bench.

"*Luojan kiitos* [Thank goodness], nothing's broken," said Anna expertly. "But it's a bad sprain." She rummaged in a cupboard and came back with a towel soaked in something so excruciatingly cold that Fredriksson's tight-lipped self-control deserted him and he whimpered like a puppy as she placed it over his foot.

Recovering, he noticed the unaccustomed smell from the towel and at first meant to protest, since he was a teetotaler and had signed the pledge. But he was a tall man and the distance seemed considerable from his foot to his conscience, which only trembled faintly in the pure fragrance of aquavit.

There wasn't a lot Torsson could do. He had to go on alone with Vuori to Rakisjokk to try to sort out the fight that had taken place. He waved off Fredriksson and the police car by the road and turned his skis toward the lake and Rakisjokk.

Henrik Vuori had not said much about what had happened when they met at Anna's that morning. Torsson had meant to question him on the way, but nothing much came of the questions and answers once they were out on the lake. They were skiing straight into the biting wind along the track to the village marked out by juniper branches. Calmly and economically, Vuori was poling his way forward at a pace that could easily become murderous unless he was planning to take a break now and then. Torsson stared steadily at his back as he sweated off the manifestations of high living beneath his skin. He began speculating on whether prolonged physical effort might result in a heart attack in somewhat overweight people. The beams from their headlamps flickered over the juniper branches in the dark.

The Rakisjaure is a long, narrow lake stretching from Keinoluokta in the east almost due west to Rakisjokk. In the summer it can lie icily calm, reflecting its sharp banks with their hanging clumps of cloudberries in its slanting, glossy eye. Rakisjokk is enclosed on three sides by mountains; the lake is its eye and lungs. The villagers have a habit of looking up toward the mountain, which is not only their largest but also the highest in the country, if they want to know what to expect in the way of weather. There are days when they can see Wolf Ridge all the way from Tuolpagorni to Kebnepakte. Then the barometer needle twitches up a couple of notches at the first light early morning tap of a knuckle. The air is like chilled wine to breathe and the thoughts of the villagers are light.

But then there are times when the mountain ridge is shrouded in heavy clouds and the sun can be perceived only as a mocking gleam in the gray. There is also a time when to the inhabitants of Rakisjokk the mountain appears to have swallowed the sun. Toward March, they start peering up at the ridges in the midday gloaming, wondering whether they will soon see the edge of it—the first blood-red inkling of an infinitely long summer day.

From the beginning—and no one knows when that was, not even the nomad-school inspector—only Sami people lived in Rakisjokk. Now, since the advent of the nomad school, Swedes have moved up the slope to measure the temperature and precipitation, to teach the children and cater to and profit from the tourists. Rakisjokk Nomad School is a school where the children receive neither fresh milk nor newspapers. Nevertheless, it has been left there to function on its own in the wilderness. The glow from the ceiling light in its upper hall was the first gleam of life Constable Torsson saw as he and Vuori approached the village in the dead, dark gray dawn over the lake.

Someone had heard them. He could see figures moving on the snow-covered jetty and a Norwegian elkhound was

8

yapping monotonously. But when they reached the jetty there was no one there to meet them. He could see the figures moving farther up now and was both annoyed and discomforted. He was as tired as only an unfit ninety-eight-kilo body could be after twenty-five kilometers on oranges and cigarettes. He longed to be in the warmth indoors, where the smell of coffee from the kettle permanently brewing on the stove would be hanging in the air. But Vuori knew nothing of exhaustion. He scraped the ice off his upper lip with his mitten and blew his nose in the air.

"We've put him in Jerf's shed," he said. He was propping his skis up against the cottage wall, because the wind was really nasty now.

"Matti?"

"Aye."

The door to Vuori's cottage slowly creaked open and a man in an Icelandic sweater and pointed Sami boots appeared on the steps.

"Hi," he said curtly.

He moved uneasily around them as they trudged up the slope, always keeping his distance. Torsson's feet felt boot-heavy and stiff without skis. The bloody elkhound wouldn't stop yapping. If only he could have seen it, but it was moving, just like the man behind them, on the edge of their vision where the darkness deepened.

Vuori thumped unnecessarily hard on the door of Per-Anders Jerf's cottage. The Sami ran what there was of the tourist office in Rakisjokk in the summer. Now, since their father had moved out, the house held only him and his sister Kristina Maria.

"Old Jerf insists on staying at the winter camp," Vuori

explained. "The children are worried about him, because it's at least four kilometers up to the Kaittas tent. Crazy old man," he added, spitting into the snow.

Per-Anders was a dark, gangling youth of no more than thirty. He moved very softly and rapidly across the snow-covered yard.

"Have you got the key to the shed?"

"Aye," said Per-Anders, slapping his breast pocket.

"You go on ahead to the school. We'll come up later," Vuori called to the man in the sweater, who had stopped outside the circle of light from the porch. Only then did Torsson realize that the man was Erik Sjögren.

They had reached the shed, and while Jerf was trying to turn the key in the creaking lock Torsson and Vuori sought shelter around the corner of the building. The wind had turned even more persistent and contained sharp snowflakes.

"Bloody locks! They kind of freeze up if you don't use them for a few days."

"It happened yesterday, didn't it?" said Torsson.

"Yesterday? Let's see, where are we . . . Wednesday. Yes, it was yesterday. You lose count sometimes up here. Got it, bastard key."

He opened the shed door and they stepped inside, lit by Jerf's torch, the beam dancing jerkily over the wooden walls. Torsson noted the unprepared reindeer skins and the stench from them; also antlers, bundles of ropes, and empty wooden crates. But the shed seemed mostly filled with the kind of things that couldn't be seen. The shifting patches of light were insufficient. The wind was nosing through the cracks and whistling greedily.

The cone of light fell on a raised blanket thrown over a provisional trestle table.

"Here he is, poor devil," said Jerf.

He pulled the blanket back, exposing a rigid face so expressionless that it seemed doubtful whether it had ever belonged to a human being. The man lying on the wooden table looked neither injured nor battered, just frozen and dead.

"Keep the torch still, Per-Anti. The constable can't see."

That was Vuori. His voice rasped like fingernails against wood, Torsson thought.

He didn't look as if he'd received a blow. What had he died of? Torsson wondered. There were no rules here. He could have died of anything. Of the darkness.

"Shut that damned dog up!"

He heard himself shouting and was ashamed. They clumped out of the shed in their heavy boots, only Jerf silent on his reindeer-skin soles. Torsson inhaled sharp snow and air through his mouth as they came out. Wasn't Vuori smiling at him?

"Yes, we're sad about the accident to our schoolmaster," Jerf said quietly.

"Oh, so it was an accident? All I was told was that he was dead."

"He's dead all right."

The words hung in the air despite the wind screaming like a demon and twisting off Jerf's ski cap.

"Wonder whether he froze to death or died from the blow?" Vuori mumbled.

"Blows can be unfortunate sometimes. The human body has vulnerable points," said Jerf. "But he looked frozen enough when we found him."

"I left my rucksack on the steps. I'll go and get it," said Vuori, pulling the flap of his cap down over his eyes.

11

"Did you get hold of anything?"

"Yes. The shopkeeper drove out to Orjas himself with the gear. The only thing he didn't have was the headmaster's candelabra candles. He left big ones instead so he'll have to whittle them down somehow. We've got a crystal candelabrum in the village, see," he added to Torsson. "The headmaster's got a crystal-glass candelabrum. It's the most beautiful thing we've got next to our English teacher."

Torsson wondered when he would be allowed to see these sights.

"Go on up to the school. I'll soon catch you up."

"And oranges, did you get them?" Jerf asked.

At the school, silence had once more enveloped Matti. Waves of small talk were now lapping over the place where he had sunk. But in the light of the lamp above the steps, Torsson saw that Jerf's cheeks were wet and wondered whether it was the cold making his eyes water.

He leaned against the wind on his way up to the schoolhouse and his ears popped. He aimed his steps toward the light and then kept his eyes down.

It came as a shock to find someone standing in front of him. Had she been blown by the wind out of a snowdrift or had she emerged from the clump of wind-twisted mountain birches? Anyway, Vuori couldn't have gone far because Torsson heard him shouting over the wind:

"This is my wife Marta. She's the matron at the school." The wind couldn't carry away the pride in his voice. "She's from Kuivakangas."

The fair-haired woman was nearly as tall as Torsson.

She was certainly twenty years younger and half a head taller than her husband.

"*Päüve* [Hello]," said the woman from Tornedal in Finnish dialect, holding out her hand.

"*Päüve,*" said Torsson and shook it. "*Tuletko sinä niin kaukana* . . . [So you come from so far . . .]" He thought he'd put it so that it sounded quite good.

"*Niin* [Aye]," she replied, and closed her mouth on her secrets. Then she was gone into the swirling gray. He put his shoulder to the wind and struggled on.

There was a dark, closed main entrance in the long wall of the school, but a light was on in the gable wall above a small door and some steps with an iron railing. Crouching against the wind, someone was unlocking the door. Torsson was already up the steps when the man straightened up, revealing a white face in the lamplight. It was Erik Sjögren. He said nothing.

It wasn't until a few seconds later that Torsson discovered they weren't alone, and he sensed rather than knew the presence of someone in the darkness. She stepped forward and the light fell on a head of hair that looked black but showed a reddish tinge when she moved. However, she moved very little. Torsson looked on her as a savior.

"Hello," he said, holding out his hand. "I'm Constable Torsson," he went on, gazing for a second or two into the gray eyes dominating the pale oval face. Perhaps she wasn't as beautiful as he had thought at first glance. But those eyes! He shuffled his booted feet and waited for her to introduce herself.

"Hello," said this Rose of the Wilderness, without proffering her hand.

The room Sjögren let them into was long and narrow,

with no vestibule. Nor was the heating on, and it felt cold and damp. Torsson wondered what the point was of receiving him there. Three workbenches stood along the window wall, and cupboards and shelves along the opposite wall were full of schoolboy Sami craftwork. Pictures were stacked in every other vacant space, panels and canvases, all of them mountain landscapes, all with summer motifs. Torsson was not knowledgeable about art, but he thought the paintings looked strange. The landscapes were in sentimental colours, a pale mauve dominating. All the skies had a green tone which made them look cold and distant. Then he spotted quite a large painting of water foaming out of rock—perhaps the stream outside.

The canvas had been destroyed. Powerful slashes with a knife had ripped and torn the linen fabric.

As long as he was alone with the two of them, there was no other sound than a rasping noise as Sjögren ran a callused hand down his stubble. The girl was sitting upright on a chair, saying nothing. Then the stamping of feet could be heard on the steps and the others came clumping in, puffing and snorting with the cold. Eklind, the headmaster, looked bizarre in this company, being dressed in overcoat, galoshes, and an astrakhan hat. He introduced Torsson to the dark-haired English teacher, Anna Ryd, and Torsson bowed clumsily from a distance, frightened by her paralyzing silence. He began to realize that it was a sign of grief.

As they stood there beneath the naked bulb, in woolen shawls and caps with earflaps, they seemed to him nothing but eyes. He couldn't keep them apart, almost confusing the dark, chubby Kristina Maria Jerf, Per-Anders's sister, with the tall Marta Vuori. They took their time scanning his face. He began to realize that he was now among the upper ten of Rakisjokk—here, however, even counting the elkhound, numbering only eight.

"Yes, well," said the headmaster in an unexpectedly light voice. "This is where it happened."

So at long last he was given an explanation. Henrik Vuori took off his cap and looked around as if wishing to assure himself of the attention of all those present.

"You see, we've asked you to come here, Constable Torsson, and caused you to make this long journey because of the great misfortune that has befallen us over Matti."

The corners of Anna Ryd's mouth hardened as if she were facing a difficult test, and Marta Vuori looked at her with an almost amused glint in her eye.

"Last Monday, Sjögren and Matti had arranged a bit of a party in the evening at their cottage," Vuori went on. "Jerf was there, and so was I. We had a few drinks . . ." He hesitated and his eyes met Per-Anders's brown ones. "Anyhow, Matti must've had a few too many. He started ranting about life up here. About the darkness and how we grate against each other. Toward the end of winter, we often get like that."

Did he understand? He thought the seven pairs of eyes turned toward him were sniffing the air like the moist noses of dogs.

"Matti was perhaps the most sensitive of us all. He got upset about everything. For some reason he went off up to the school and into the craft room here, and Erik Sjögren followed to see what he was up to. When he got here, Matti was quite beside himself and was attacking his pictures with a sheath knife. Matti had the gift of painting, as you know."

He paused to allow them to consider that gift.

15

"The pictures he'd done were the best things he owned. Otherwise he didn't bother much about what he'd got or hadn't got. Erik tried to stop him, of course. But Matti turned furiously angry and tried to damage Erik's model, which he kept in here. Now, that model is Erik's most precious possession—"

"What kind of model?"

Sjögren looked up with light, dreamy eyes, a sober edge around the iris. "It's supposed to be a meteorological observation instrument," he said quietly. "It's a model I've made from my own designs and ideas."

Henrik Vuori raised his voice as he went on. "It's a sort of invention. Erik snatched the knife out of Matti's hand, but he wouldn't let go and in the end Erik had to hit him on the chin. It wasn't all that hard a blow, but Matti collapsed. As everyone realizes, the blow was necessary. Erik picked up the model and carried it back to his cottage. Jerf and I had gone home by then, but he sat down and had another couple of drinks. When Matti didn't come back, he went up to the school to look for him. But he'd gone. Erik switched off the lights and closed the craft-room door behind him, because it'd been left open, and then he went home to bed. He didn't bother to find out where Matti had gone; he thought he'd be back."

Vuori gazed searchingly at Sjögren for a moment or two, with a look of pity, then went on.

"So this morning, yesterday morning, I mean, we found Matti outside the school. He was lying in the snow, dead. I suppose he froze to death. Drunk as he was, he must have fallen over and passed out."

"Who found him?"

There was silence, and it surprised Torsson that their

eyes never wavered. In the end, Per-Anders Jerf put a hand up to his cropped hair.

"I did."

"When?"

"I was going up the mountain to see to some reindeer that I'd heard had got themselves into a spot they couldn't get down from. So I took the track behind the school—"

"*Miksi sinä niin sanot? Pidähän varasi.* [Why say that? Watch out.]" A brief, low-voiced warning from the dark, chubby one Torsson took to be Kristina Maria, the sister.

Jerf was drawing invisible figures with the points of his Sami boots on the floor and looked confused.

"The constable speaks as good Finnish as you do," Marta Vuori remarked in her Kuivakangas dialect. She smiled a crooked smile which did not get as far as her eyes. Kristina Maria put her hands to her pursed mouth and laughed. She switched to Sami and turned to Jerf with a long cooing sentence, her brown eyes playing on Torsson, who could understand nothing.

Despite his anger, he felt ill at ease. The feeling was so concrete that he had to swallow a wave of nausea. As if in telepathic communication with the nerves of his stomach, the elkhound started barking outside.

"Well, as I was saying," Jerf went on, "I went past the school and saw a figure slumped in the snow just below the craft-room steps. He was covered with snow, but I pulled him up and saw it was Matti. Well, he was dead. So I put my skis back on and went to find someone. The first person I met was Anna Ryd on her way across the school-yard. When she heard what had happened, she went there, of course. And she was crying . . ."

He fell silent.

1 7

"What time was it you went out?"

"Just before eight, I think, because I switched off the morning service when I left the kitchen."

Torsson turned to Anna Ryd. He wanted to hear her speak. "When did you last see him?"

"Who?" she asked hoarsely.

"Matti Olsson."

He might just as well have hit her. She fell forward against the workbench and wept silently, her back shaking.

"Oh, well," said Torsson awkwardly, "I understand how you feel."

She jerked upright, suddenly clear-eyed. "You certainly don't," she replied, her eyes as hard as snow crust. "I met him for a moment on the evening before he went to his house, to that . . . party. He'd been up to see Edvin Jerf in the Kaittas tent with coffee and tobacco. He stopped at my place for about five minutes."

"What were you doing in the schoolyard in the morning?"

He wasn't going to let her go, not yet.

"I was on my way to school. I was in a hurry because I had a lesson at half past eight."

"What were the rest of you doing? That evening, I mean."

Eklind looked as if he had been waiting for his moment. He straightened up. "We were playing mah-jongg," he said in the matter-of-fact tone of a schoolmaster, using the minimum of air.

Torsson's pen stopped moving, at a loss. His shorthand system did not allow for Chinese words.

"Mah-jongg," said the loose-limbed figure in the chair very distinctly. "A fine old family game. We always play it here in Rakisjokk in the winter. When all the books have been read, all subjects of conversation exhausted . . ." His childlike blue eyes eagerly sought Torsson's. "It's so simple. Or rather, it *looks* so complicated. You have to learn all the different hands. But once you've learned them, it's astonishingly simple. However"—thirty years of teaching lay behind the raised forefinger—"that's where you're mistaken, after all." He smiled triumphantly. "You find that the possible combinations are innumerable. There are all kinds of fine points and complications."

He leaned forward and lowered his voice. "I've once sat on nine tiles."

Mad as a hatter, Torsson thought nervously. But the others were just as serious. They're all mad, he thought fleetingly.

"And," said Eklind with clear emphasis, "I've had the Big Three Dragons hand."

"Er . . . really?" said Torsson. "That must be quite something."

"I'm convinced," Eklind went on, sinking back on his wooden chair as best he could, "that before my time is up, I'll experience at least Earthly Harmony."

"Let's hope so," Torsson put in loudly; "that sounds very nice." But he didn't think it sounded nice. "Now to this business about Matti Olsson. That's not exactly harmony. Did you see him that evening?"

"No, I told you—we were playing mah-jongg in here, Kristina Maria, Marta, Anna, and I."

"In here?"

Not that it would surprise him if they had sat in a freezing craft room in their tranquil madness.

"No, in the hall next door. There's an open fireplace in the school hall, so we often sit there in the evenings. We'd stopped long ago when it happened. We quit playing when I got the Big Three Dragons hand. I left the tiles on the table so that the children could see what I had experienced. I hadn't seen Matti since about seven that evening. He was up at Anna's when he came back from Kaittas and was presumably on his way home again."

"Did he seem upset or unhappy, or in any other way out of the ordinary?"

This question, stepping stiffly straight out of the pages of the interrogation manual, made seven pairs of eyes turn toward Torsson.

"No," said Eklind. "To be honest, he was a bit rude, that's all. He didn't even say hello, although he'd been away all afternoon."

"When did he go to Kaittas?"

"About one o'clock, I think."

"So he didn't have any lessons that afternoon?"

"What?" said Eklind. "No, he didn't."

"His day off, was it?"

"No, not exactly. We aren't all that formal here."

Someone—and it wasn't Torsson—suddenly decided the questioning was over. Just how that happened he didn't have time to take in. But there was a stamping of boots and scattered remarks about the raw cold in the room.

"Bloody cold," said Per-Anders Jerf, moving toward the door.

Torsson might just as well have tried to stop an avalanche, but he did manage to call Erik Sjögren back. Torsson stood stroking the handle of a knife with one hand, one of the craftwork products. It had a smooth and friendly surface.

"What did it look like in here when you finally came back?" he said.

"Same as now." He did not lower his eyes.

"When did you come back?"

"Must have been after one."

"You didn't see Matti in the snow then?"

"What?" said Sjögren stupidly. "No, I didn't see anything. It's dark here."

Torsson went over to the door and opened it. They went out together and got the full blast of the wind in their faces.

"Where was he lying?"

"Over there." He pointed straight down below the drainpipe on the corner of the building.

"Well," said Torsson, "that's all for the time being. Are you going home?"

"I'm going into the school hall. The others are there, I think."

"Good," said Torsson, his nose deep inside his coat collar. He had snow in his ears and eyes and the inside of his wet scarf felt disagreeable. "Then I can ask you about something in there."

Sjögren turned quickly around and Torsson caught a glint in his eye in the darkness. "What? Anything special?"

"Well," said Torsson, "special? That depends. It's about the blood."

"The blood?"

Torsson could see only his back, but there was profound circumspection in his voice.

"Oh, aye, on the picture and the floor in front of it. He cut himself on the knife, see. He cut himself quite badly

21

when we were fighting over the knife," he repeated monotonously.

"So he cut himself on the knife. And you knocked him unconscious."

Torsson was speaking searchingly as if trying to see the scene in front of him.

"And yet," he went on more quickly, "and yet you didn't go back until a couple of hours later to see how he was."

"No, I didn't."

Sjögren hunched up against the wind and had his hands deep in his pockets as he walked away. His footsteps were inaudible in his reindeer-skin boots in the new snow.

Torsson dozed on Henrik Vuori's kitchen bench that night. He listened to the windowpanes rattling and a door that kept slamming far away. Had Jerf forgotten to lock the door of his shed?

Morning came, as pitch dark and imperceptible as other winter mornings. And yet there was a great difference. The people of Rakisjokk faced the day with glistening eyes, almost as if it had given them a touch of fever. The restlessness infected even the dogs. They ran barking to and fro outside the schoolhouse while the children sang, "The bright sun again arises," carefully articulating the difficult Swedish words and making the windowpanes vibrate.

With twenty minutes left to go, the children were already bunched together in front of the schoolhouse. The boys wore traditional Sami tunics in honor of the day and the girls were stiff and quiet in their tinkling silver ornaments. The little group of seven people Torsson had met in the craft room were huddled together in the yard with Torsson in the middle. He too was staring fixedly at the curve of the mountain ridge outlined in sharp contour against the clear sky. His eyes were smarting from staring so hard and from the increasingly bright light beginning to creep up behind the mountain. The sky looked cold, a sharp green tone slowly absorbing the first red tinge. The upturned faces were grave, eyes rarely blinking as they followed the struggle of the red light against the cold sky.

This was the moment they all had marked in their diaries. The snow stopped creaking, nothing moved in the schoolyard. The rounded, blood-red edge of the sun showed itself above the distant mountain ridge.

Vuori's elkhound broke the silence, raising its nose in the air toward the light and letting out a long-drawn-out howl.

"Shut up, will you!" Vuori yelled.

"He can't stand the sun!"

A boy in the highest form had called out and his remark was greeted with a burst of laughter. The next moment, fifteen children were tumbling around in the snow, their hands covering their eyes.

"We can't stand the sun!" cried the girls. "We'll burn! Matron, can we have some suntan oil? It's burning like fire!"

They choked with laughter and slapped snow-wet hands over each other's eyes.

"I realize it burns your maidenly skins," said Vuori. "Look at Ibb-Kajsa, her nose has gone all freckled."

More laughter, and snowballs began swirling through the air. In the tumult, Torsson noticed Eklind, the headmaster. He was standing quite still, staring at the dazzling edge of the sun. His glasses had misted over and tears were running fast and silently down his chapped, freshly shaved cheeks.

Twilight descended swiftly again. The faces that had brightened in the red light once more turned pale and rather serious. The twilight came as a great disappointment for most of them, as if they'd thought they could get the sun to stay by yelling and hallooing, rather like stopping a kitchen clock by holding the pendulum.

A bunch of children gathered in front of Torsson. "Are you a policeman?"

"Aye," he replied self-consciously. "Of course. Yes, I am."

"Did they phone you to say Matti was dead?"

"That's why I'm here," he replied evasively.

"I told you so," said one boy, feet planted wide in Sami boots. "They said he'd gone to town on Sunday and then that he'd had an accident. But we know he's lying in Per-Anti's shed."

The next moment the speaker darted behind the backs of three girls and there was a lot of tittering.

"We haven't had any crafts or drawing for three days. Wonder what'll happen to us?"

A machine-gun fire of Sami interrupted the bold one. The bunch moved away. Torsson reckoned the boy was being reprimanded for joking about Matti's death. Girls in general have a more subtle feeling for the faux pas of conversation.

Slowly, Torsson hauled himself up the craft-room steps and felt the door. It was not locked, so he went in. The cold air inside smelled of turpentine and new wood. He no longer knew what he was looking for. The bloodstains on the floor no longer looked significant in the sober winter dusk.

At the far end of the room was a door and three steps leading to the school hall. He could hear the murmur of voices from the other side as he stood flicking through a stack of Matti's canvases by the door. It looked as if Matti had focused on the same birch tree and the same bit of boggy ground in painting after painting. As he touched the last canvas leaning against the wall, something fell to the floor. He heard a light clatter, but his own shadow stopped him seeing what it was. He moved around and peered in among the wet tracks left by his boots.

There it was. He bent down and picked the object up, then turned it round and round between his great thumb and forefinger. He had no idea what it was supposed to be. It was a small rectangle, hardly bigger than two sugar lumps. The back was neatly rounded and made of some kind of light-colored wood—he guessed bamboo when he saw the narrow capillaries where it had been cut across. The front was of bone and had a green squiggle on it. It looked like a Chinese character.

He would have dumped the object on a shelf and gone away if it hadn't been for the spots of blood forming an asymmetrical pattern on the white bone.

At that moment he distinguished a voice in the muffled noise from the hall on the other side of the door. It was Marta Vuori speaking rapidly and loudly in Finnish. He pictured her with some color in her cheeks—her voice sounded scornful and excited. He caught one single word before a burst of laughter from the others drowned the sound of her voice. ". . . *mestarisalapoliisistako!*"

A long and cumbersome construction in Finnish: "from

the master detective"? He had heard it before at some time or other. He swiftly pressed the door handle down. The door was locked.

The laughter inside ceased abruptly. Torsson let go of the door handle and it sprang up with a click. A low titter came from inside.

"Oh, hell!" said Torsson between his teeth, anger pumping blood into his face. He put the little object with the Chinese character into his trouser pocket and closed his hand around it.

An hour later, as Torsson poled his way down the slope toward the lake, he no longer had a shadow. He had switched on his headlamp and it was flickering uneasily on Erik Sjögren's back. Sjögren was skiing with his head down, for the wind had unfortunately turned and was now blowing off the lake. Torsson glanced over his shoulder to see whether Henrik Vuori was keeping up.

Indeed, Vuori was skiing onward as doggedly now as he had on the way there from Orjas. He was pulling the sledge, which made a rustling noise as it slid through the loose snow. They had lashed the sailcloth around Matti's body and pulled the blanket over his face. The sledge was jerking and jumping in the tracks.

2 . DAVID DOES NOT FIND LOVE

They say all roads lead to Rome.

He could just see the self-satisfied expression of some platitudinous medieval pensioner chewing over this piece of wisdom in his toothless mouth. For the road he was now traveling led to a place called Orjas and absolutely nowhere else on earth. According to the map, it came to an end right there. He had already experienced the delights of driving along the most northerly road in the world, and the car's painstakingly taped headlights showed that he also expected it to be the worst. But he had never before been on a road that did not lead to Rome or any place other than Orjas.

Occasionally the road seemed to be leading to heaven, the car climbing in growling second gear up kilometer-long hills toward the empty sky. Since his career as a driver was not significantly longer in duration than the four weeks he had owned the car, he was entering deeply into the engine's achievements. He was leaning forward, groaning slightly as it climbed steeply upward. When he reached the top of what had hitherto been the worst hill, the landscape appeared to slope down forever toward Rakisjaure. From there he saw, for the first time, what he had partly come for: high, snow-capped mountains.

This July day was clear, the sky blue. The mountains seemed to him to be the most immobile and largest objects he had ever seen. Top marks to you, old chap, he thought, for David Malm travels around the world, painting, and he's seen a thing or two, the Eiffel Tower as well as the Grand Hotel in Sveg.

He was glad he was on his own so he didn't have to articulate this. Instead he made music, which was easier. Over and over again, he whistled the same flamenco tune, tapping his free left foot in time against the rubber mat. As he sat there whistling as loudly and out of tune as a solitary person can, he had his very first encounter on his way to Orjas. Initially he couldn't think what it was that was coming toward him in the middle of the road at a languorous jog trot. Then he saw it was his first ever reindeer and it was smaller than he had thought they would be.

The creature, a male with fully grown antlers, seemed confused by the sight of the car and decided to stop. David Malm braked and managed to stop about five meters in front of the reindeer, now standing looking at him with watchful brown eyes. It did not move.

Hands trembling, David extracted his camera from the glove compartment, adjusted it to a sixteen stop and 1/125th second's exposure, then cautiously opened the car door. He got out and prepared to take a photo. But the moment the reindeer's gaze met the vacant stare of the lens, it veered away and vanished across the road through the soft crowberry shrubs. Its white rump gleamed for a few moments among the pines, then it was gone. Once more the silence all around was like the Monday morning of the Creation.

He had been told that reindeer had a beautiful gait and was disappointed. This chap had been lolloping along like a bewildered cow. It wasn't until he had started the car up again and for the first time mastered the art of driving while smoking a pipe that it occurred to him—right hindquarters. That peculiar gait. The creature had been hurt.

He had hardly had time to get used to that thought when he noticed a crashed car on the other side of the road. Its radiator was squashed into a rock on the verge. It was a brand-new, sky-blue Volkswagen, a twin to his own.

"Little sister," he murmured, "little sister! That's the way the cookie crumbles."

He drove up to the verge and stopped. (He had to admire himself for this: stopping, swinging around, backing, changing gear, and doing practically everything that, generally speaking, can be done with a car. Like Juan Fangio's younger brother.) But there were no skid marks in the gravel. The road was as straight as the parting in a lecturer's hair. Why had that car swerved and driven off the road?

He went over to it and looked through the side window. (I'll scream if I see blood, he thought.) The car was empty and a carelessly stubbed-out cigarette lay reeking in the ashtray. All around him was quiet, a cupola of seven-league silence. Inside, the thin column of smoke curled up toward the ceiling.

Cigarette, car, someone in the proximity. He was a whiz at drawing conclusions. Carried away, he drew another and looked at the front of the car for confirmation. Stiff, white reindeer hairs were stuck to the right-hand headlight in the greasy road dust.

Knees giving slightly with caution and tension, he went around the big rock and made his way into the forest. In there, the spruces had black lichen on them and the mosquitoes were shaping up for their first mass attack. He needed go no farther than a few steps over the sagging, boggy tussocks before he had his confirmation. No sound betrayed her, neither a sob nor a twig breaking. Only the white glint of a blouse.

She was sitting hunched up against a tree, as still as an animal, her gray eyes gazing at him observantly. A strand of dark hair had fallen out of the bun and spread over her shoulder. Oddly enough, he was the one who was scared.

How did she take it? God knows. She didn't smile as people usually did when David Malm appeared in his stained linen jacket and stiff corduroy trousers that made a sibilant noise with every step. Just because he felt scared and stupid and dazzled (white blouse and beauty), he called out like a scoutmaster, "Hi there! So there you are!"

She got up and carefully brushed down her skirt, but her eyes didn't leave his face for a moment. Then she started walking purposefully toward the car. He had no idea whether this control was hiding shock.

"Why did you creep in there?" he cried.

She turned around and a moment went by before she replied. He was to learn that this observant circumspection was characteristic.

"I was frightened."

As if talking about someone else. She walked on.

"You . . . you hit a reindeer."

"I know."

She had reached the car now, and with a slight frown was examining the dented front.

"You can't drive that," he said helpfully. "Bust."

"I could if someone would pull out the bumper for me. It's jammed against the wheel. But that looks impossible."

She was scrutinizing him as if he were a naked model. At that moment he would willingly have lifted a whole house, family and all, for her, but he declined. In truth, it probably was impossible.

"You can come with me."

"But you're going to Orjas."

"I can turn back. It doesn't matter. I'll get there eventually. And you have to report to the police that you've hit a reindeer. I saw it. It was injured."

Where did his officiousness come from?

"Oh," she said slowly, "it was a stray, one of Stig Anders's. I can tell him."

No, she had another and more serious problem, he could see that from the small frown.

"I'll turn around and give you a lift. Where were you going? To town?"

"No," she said suddenly and harshly. "I was getting out of here . . . going down south. Traveling . . ."

"Far?"

"Yes, a long way away."

"But you have to report it," he persisted. "And besides, you have to get the car fixed."

"Yes. Strange . . . this has made me feel so calm."

She wasn't talking to him, that was for sure. He was redheaded and his eyes were popping with agitation and zeal. With a great effort, he managed to put on a more virile expression. She didn't notice the transformation.

"Where are you going?" she asked.

"To—what the hell is it called? Rakisjokk. You get there by boat."

She nodded as if she knew the place.

"Do you know the people there? I'm going to see a good friend of mine. His name's Matti," said David eagerly. "It's a whole year since he invited me, I know, but then I went to Spain instead. But he'll be at home; he never leaves the village in summer, so I'm told. Do you know if he's still painting? You see, Matti could really paint . . ."

To this stumbling outpouring she had but one answer. Her eyes searched his sweaty face with curiosity.

"Matti's dead."

They say that; in a life-threatening situation or after a severe shock such as a blow from behind, a person somehow notices the most trivial of details. He saw that her lips bore traces of pink lipstick when she smiled, only slightly and with a hint of scorn when she spoke.

"Dead?"

"Yes, dead," she said impatiently. "Six months ago now. No, not quite. Back in March."

"How . . . did he die?"

"He was drunk and got into a fight, then went and lay down in a snowdrift. Of his own free will."

This was when the grief hit him, and the only way he could express it was to shout straight into that hateful face, "Who are you, anyway?"

She was still smiling, rather fixedly. "My name's Anna Ryd."

"Did you know Matti?"

Again that reflective pause before she replied, "No, I didn't."

Then she surprised him by adding, like a friendly comment intended just for him, "I only thought I did."

David pulled himself together. "I'll take you to town," he said. "And I'm going to take you to the police whether you like it or not. You're obliged to report that reindeer. Where's your luggage? I'll transfer it to my car."

"It doesn't matter," she said. For someone in shock, she was looking very determined.

"You can't leave your luggage in the car."

He opened the car door and looked inside. There was a strange little object dumped on the passenger seat. It looked like something out of a folk museum, and although he had never seen anything like it before, he knew at once what it was: a birch-bark knapsack.

Anna Ryd opened the car door on the other side and grabbed the quaint bag. Then she headed for his car. David released the lock and went around and raised the hood. But the luggage compartment was empty. There had been nothing else in the car except the girl and the birch-bark knapsack.

A U-turn in a street was something he had not entirely mastered when taking his driving test, but he had got away with it. Turning on a gravel road was much the same thing raised to the power of three. After he had backed four times, the girl beside him finally lost control.

"Get out and I'll turn it for you!"

Of course it didn't matter to her that his male self-image had been dealt a mortal blow. Oddly enough, neither was he all that bothered. He was thinking about Matti.

Of his own free will, she had said. The words grated on him like pink against purple. They were untrue and he knew it. Matti, the dreamer, had been as sensitive as a barometer needle, vibrating and swinging back and forth. But the idea that he would voluntarily have lain down to die in a snowdrift was preposterous.

"Of his own free will, you said." The words escaped him suddenly. "I don't believe it."

They had changed places at the wheel again, the sun now flashing in the rearview mirror.

"He loved life."

He could hear how gushingly bathetic it sounded. But she replied unsmilingly, "Not all lives."

Her words took his breath away and he said nothing for the rest of the way. In fact he surprised himself, because it was thirty kilometers back to town and he couldn't remember ever keeping silent for so long in a waking state. The profile beside him was beautiful and expressionless.

They drove into the mining town that squatted between the ore mountains. Their first view of it was from slightly above. Reflections of the sun flashed off the roofs of the houses, which still looked half finished or newly built. It was easy to imagine the town being abandoned any day, leaving behind a scrap heap of boards and tiles between the two rounded mountains. Yet the flashes of sunlight would still leap as happily from roof to roof in the silence. David's good mood returned without his noticing it. He couldn't help it, and it didn't mean he had forgotten Matti. He had just pushed him further into his mind for the moment.

It amused him that he knew where the police station was so that he didn't have to ask her. He put the engine into neutral on the steep hill leading down to it and let the car roll just to show what a Fangio he was after all.

"You stay in the car," he ordered, his spirits raised by this test of his manhood. He strode into the police station, his jacket tails flapping in the dry, fusty air. The next moment he bumped into a police officer in the process of pulling on his uniform jacket. The enterprise demanded great care since the two pieces in front would hardly meet across his stomach. He was sweating profusely from the effort. When he finally had the jacket properly buttoned up, it lay decoratively in spare tires around his waist and the spaces between the buttons had become oval cracks. Ready, he turned his light blue eyes on David.

"Excuse me," said David humbly. He gazed around the corridor, registering the pinched atmosphere. Officialdom in Sweden, he established, was best expressed through pale green paint and stainless steel.

"I'm a poor retarded man," he began his speech to the police authorities of this mining town. "I have a girl in my car. She's as beautiful as she's . . . wicked." To his annoyance, he noticed his voice sliding out of the part. But he improved on it. "I'm afraid it's all too much for me. Would you save me from her?"

The large policeman looked at him. "Aye," he said.

Then he sighed heavily, with the result that a button

came away from his jacket and flew, official insignia and all, past David's ear to land with a metallic click on the floor. The constable cleared his throat.

"No one injured, I hope," he said.

"No one."

"Let's go out and take a look at her," the constable said calmly. "My name's Torsson. Do you know what your name is?"

"Yes."

"That's good."

Out in the car, Anna Ryd was still sitting with her forbidding profile toward the entrance to the police station. Torsson stopped on the steps and peered at her.

"Huh," was all he said.

The girl turned and David saw her stiffening. Then she got out of the car and he almost applauded the first sign of emotion he had seen on her face.

"Miss Ryd," the constable said slowly. "Well, well."

She said nothing, her mouth tightening. David, of course, couldn't stop himself.

"Known to the police already?" he said. "Then I'm off."

"Oh, no," said Torsson, without taking his eyes off the girl. "You stay here."

"I stay here," David agreed, mimicking his singsong way of speaking. "And how long do we have to stay here taking in the sight of one another?" He shifted his weight.

"I've crashed my car," the girl said coolly. "It was brand new, I'd bought it for my holiday and left it at Anna's in Orjas. I ran into one of the stray reindeer and swerved into a rock. I don't think the reindeer was badly hurt. I meant to tell Stig Anders myself, because it's his reindeer that run there, but this . . . gentleman insisted we should go to the police."

"Allow me to introduce myself," said David. "Cub Scout David Malm. Dib dib dib."

"Oh, stop playing the fool," said the girl.

He smiled with delight. She really was out of kilter now.

"Can't," he said. "I'm like that."

"Retarded," said Torsson quietly and calmly. The girl's eyes widened in surprise.

"You have a whole register of different expressions," David observed.

"Let's go inside." The big policeman took her by the elbow and piloted her up the steps. "Wait here for the time being," he said to David. "I'll deal with you later."

"I have a feeling I'm going to get eight years for this," he said meekly.

"Or the loony bin."

The girl glanced over her shoulder as he got into the car and sat down. She looked almost as if she wanted to go back, but changed her mind. He started filling his pipe and thinking about her. The birch-bark bag, of course. She'd wanted to take it when she saw he was staying in the car. And yet it looked as if she hadn't wanted to take it with her into the police station. She thinks I'm a gentleman after all, he thought. She thinks.

He began to examine the bag. So this was what she took with her for a long journey, was it? A long way away, down south, she'd said. He couldn't help being curious about its contents and started filling it in his imagination: toothbrush, a pale green nylon nightie, a bound copy of *New Yoga: Control and Peace of Mind*.

In the end, he became so intensely curious and the sun was blazing so hotly on the roof that he started having visions. He was also so hungry that his stomach was contracting. Maybe she had a sandwich in the bag, he thought unexpectedly. Glancing up at the entrance to the police station (he would not have liked that glance even in the snake house at the zoo), he cautiously picked up the knapsack and lifted the lid. A rope, he thought. Silly!

He started pulling at it. It was a long rope, so long that his hands became damp with sweat. He kept one eye on the entrance. Finally he had it in his lap. At the end was a loop, a wide loop not achieved with a slip knot in the rope, but formed by the rope running through a piece of bone with two holes in it. The loop had been cut through in a way that must have taken a long time to do. Why was the rope so long? he thought confusedly, suppressing his nausea. A lasso, he answered himself, it's a lasso or a lassoo or whatever it's called. Swallowing, he quickly turned the bag upside down. A collection of peculiar silver ornaments fell into his lap. Fumbling, he started stuffing the rope and the tinkling ornaments back again. He fastened the lid and sank back in the seat, breathing out.

But he couldn't shake the thought of that noose with the piece of bone. There were strands of hair in it. One of them had come loose and showed up dark against his grubby shirt cuff. It wasn't dark brown like hers, with reddish highlights. It was jet black and dead straight. But it was human hair.

3. AN ORIGINAL, HANDMADE DAVID MALM

Quite high up on the north wall of the police station was a small barred window in the smooth brick facade, and out of this window a head was protruding, manifesting almost southern enthusiasm.

"Hey, you, miss! Look over here! Hey, lads . . . phwooarr! Cop a load of that!"

But Anna Ryd did not turn her head as she marched

out of the station. "Marched" was exactly the right word, David thought. She looked like one of Cromwell's Ironsides on the march.

"If only I could've thought up such compliments for you," he sighed, smiling sourly.

"Help! Help! I'm overcome!" yelled the man in the window, somehow managing to get his hands out through the bars and press them against his dark sideburns.

"Be quiet, Sture," said Torsson mildly from his post up on the steps. "You'll embarrass the lady."

Anna Ryd opened the car door and grabbed the bark bag.

"Have you got your things?" Torsson called out. "I mean toothbrush and so on. Can I help?"

"Thanks, I've got everything here," she replied, slapping the knapsack.

Swiftly, without looking at David, she walked away. They both watched her disappearing up the hill to the hotel. The man behind bars squealed like a madman.

"Ugh," said David.

"What?"

"That girl won't be cleaning her teeth tonight." He joined Torsson on the steps.

Holding the door open for him, Torsson said calmly, "No, she probably just wanted to get rid of us. She hadn't got a toothbrush with her."

"How do you know that?"

They were inside in the smell of official forms again.

"Why should she? She was only trying out the car."

"Is that what she said?"

"Aye."

Torsson opened the door to a small stuffy room containing a desk, and let David in.

"That reindeer," he said as he sank down behind the desk. "Maybe it's not too bad. Did you see it?"

"I did. And it didn't look that badly hurt."

"I've phoned all the same. They'll see to it. And you were supposed to be going to Rakisjokk," he said. "There's no boat leaving from Orjas this evening. The girl'll have to stay in town too."

"So she's going back?"

"Of course." He looked up at David, his blue gaze inquisitive.

"I was going there," said David hestitantly, "to visit a friend of mine. Matti Olsson."

A distinct look of interest came into those blue eyes.

"But she said . . . he was dead. Strangely enough, she seemed to enjoy telling me," David burst out.

"You're wrong about that," Torsson said calmly.

"Oh, no, I'm not."

"I saw her myself just after it happened. She was" — He was searching for words — "paralyzed, yes, that's what she was."

But he was talking to himself.

"What do you mean?"

"Paralyzed with grief," he said, then suddenly smiled as if after months of thinking he'd come up with the expression.

"Oh, balls!" said David roughly. "Do you know what happened? She tried to get me to believe that he . . . that he . . ." But he couldn't say it.

"Was he a close friend of yours?"

"Yes," said David, swallowing. "Yes, he was. I haven't known him all that long, though. He was down in Stockholm last year, all winter. I think that was the only time he spent down south. He went to the same art school as I did.

He was good. Everyone believed in him. Then he went back in the summer to that stupid teaching job he had up here."

"Stupid?" Torsson repeated dreamily.

"Yes, of course," David spat. "What happened? Tell me."

"Well, you see, he got drunk one evening and started spouting about life and the darkness—"

"The darkness?"

"Yes, the darkness." Torsson looked up with a strange little smile. "You wouldn't know anything about that. He's been dead as long as that fly," he said abruptly, pointing at the shriveled corpse of a fly with its legs in the air between the two windowpanes.

"Now listen, don't be so disgusting!" David leaped up from his chair.

"I can see that you were fond of him," said the constable simply, and David began to realize how absurd the situation was. He tried to think about the police station in Klara in Stockholm, but the thought slid away.

"Well, now," said Torsson, puffing so that his stomach rose. "He got into a fight with a man called Erik Sjögren. The thing is, Matti was trying to destroy his own paintings. Sjögren stopped him. A little later he went out and lay down in a snowdrift and froze to death."

"No!" David shouted. "No, he didn't!" A knot of nerves was winding around in his stomach.

"See, he was drunk," said Torsson. "That's the way it was."

David breathed deeply to calm himself down.

"There's been a police investigation," Torsson went on, twiddling a pen between his fingers. "There was no reason to charge Sjögren with anything. None. End of story."

Torsson clasped his hands over his stomach and looked down.

"Now leave," he burst out suddenly. "Now you know what happened. Would you please go away!"

A sudden rage had begun pounding in his temples and the look he gave David was sullen. Nonetheless, David sensed that the rage was not directed at him, and the knowledge induced a strange calm in him. He made no move to go.

"Can you read shorthand?" Torsson almost roared.

"Yes, strangely enough, I can. An aunt of mine once wanted me to go into commerce. I—"

But that didn't interest Torsson. With a "Take a look at this," he cut him short and out of a desk drawer pulled a bundle of scribbled-on papers. "This is the record of the interrogations in Rakisjokk. Every word I wrote down then. Naturally you may not see the transcript, but I kept these notes. Read them if you can."

The bundle landed with a thud on the desk in front of David.

"Well, why the hell don't you take them? Since I'm crazy enough to offer. Since I've gone so totally and completely bonkers! Make the most of it."

David snatched up the bundle of papers and headed for the door.

"You had them ready to hand," he said. "Almost out on the desk."

"Get out!" the constable managed to say. "You must give them back. And when you've read them, you must tell me if there's anything I've forgotten. Do you hear? You're to tell me if there's anything I've forgotten."

People must grow peculiar up here, David thought timidly as he slipped out of the door. What was it he had babbled on about darkness? The man had at first appeared to be quite calm and sensible.

He hid the papers inside his jacket as he slipped along the corridor and grinned foolishly at a tall, bony policeman standing in a doorway with his head cocked. He must have heard Torsson's bellow. Must be crazy, David thought.

About the reindeer, not much had been said.

David went up to the hotel and asked for the same room he'd had the previous night.

"So you never got away, Mr. Malm?" said the porter, his face crinkling into worried prune creases.

"As you can see," said David curtly.

He was given back his long, narrow room with its pale gray wallpaper, and immediately flopped down on the bed with the policeman's papers in his hand. He had quite forgotten his hunger. His statement that he could read shorthand had been something of an exaggeration, he found. Moreover, Torsson had scribbled some incomprehensible hieroglyphics which he must have invented himself.

Three hours later, his neck stiff, David got off the bed. By then he'd read it all. His hunger came back and was growling at him in recognition. He was also dying for a drink. That was very unusual. He seldom drank alcohol, for the simple reason that he couldn't afford to and he had a low tolerance. But now there was this Matti business. There isn't that much drink in the world, he realized suddenly.

In the hotel dining room, an Italian three-man orchestra was tootling that summer's hits. Melancholy men in gray flannel, they must have been regretting coming to the tundra. The great dining-room windows were specially constructed to enable tourists to have their desire for sun satisfied. But most were slightly repelled by the pale midnight sunlight and wished the windows were small and leaded. As the evening was not too far gone, the atmosphere was lively. Loud-voiced men in plaid flannel shirts were drinking metallic brandy and stamping out Italian rhythms with their feet. There was only one girl in the dining room. She was with a group of engineers who were eating, drinking, talking about drilling methods, and abandoning her to the looks and inebriated comments from all around her.

The headwaiter, his face yellow from some old grievance, appeared in front of David and scrutinized his linen jacket and corduroy trousers.

"I'm sorry," said David humbly. "I don't possess a red plaid shirt."

The headwaiter decided not to love him, a decision requiring no great spiritual struggle.

"A table for one?" he asked silkily.

"No, thanks," said David hastily. "No need. I have an acquaintance here."

He hurried across the floor to a window table and the sturdy figure overflowing the chair. Out of uniform, Torsson looked naked and youthful. He had a touching specimen of bad taste below his collar—a tie with bright yellow and blue stars on a white background. He was sitting there stroking this monstrosity with a loving finger.

"Don't tease that tie," said David quietly in his ear. "It might leap up and strangle you."

Torsson turned his head stiffly. "Thanks," he said. "My name's Bengt."

David didn't ask if he might join him, but sat down. "I've read it all."

Torsson made a painful grimace. "May I have it back?" he said brusquely.

"Of course. Soon."

"Are you eating?"

"Uh-huh."

The headwaiter was swaying like a cobra above his head.

"Veal schnitzel," said David, placing a paint-stained forefinger on the menu.

"Sorry," said the headwaiter with some pleasure. "It's off. None left, I have to tell you."

"Steak."

"Sorr—"

"Char or reindeer steak," Torsson interrupted impatiently. "You must know that much."

"Reindeer steak," David said.

The headwaiter made a note of his liquid requirements, then swayed away.

"Give me the toughest, most horrible old reindeer that ever ran around eating disgusting moss," David said into the air. "I won't complain."

"Moss," said Torsson with annoyance. "Lichen! You can have them as a salad."

"Don't let's talk about it anymore. I've read it, I told you. And I'm perfectly satisfied. Let's say that I agree that you found out how my friend Matti died. Let's say that."

Torsson said nothing, but he was pained. David was not sure how to go on, so decided to wait until he had had a drink. Meanwhile Torsson told him he was eating out to celebrate the start of his holiday.

"Tomorrow," he said, throwing up his eyes. "I'm off tomorrow."

"Where to?"

"Eskilstuna." He spoke the name as if it were Las Palmas. "That's where I come from."

"I can hear that," said David.

"You can't!"

"Sometimes. Though you mostly singsong the way they do up here."

"Aye." Torsson sucked in air between his front teeth in the Sami way. "You learn."

Their drinks came. David closed his eyes and gave himself up to them. Then he spoke quickly. "You heard that I'll agree you've found out how—"

"Yes, yes. I heard."

"Good. But there's one thing I don't go along with."

Torsson's half-closed eyes betrayed no interest.

"*When* did he die?"

The orchestra had taken the opportunity to have a rest, and a temporary cessation in activities around them meant that David's words echoed from one wall to the other.

"Pardon?" said the headwaiter with a smile from above.

Marinated herring was placed on their plates. David counted eenie-meenie-minie-mo among the bits of bread and the constable calmly offered him butter. Once again they were on their own. Torsson was waiting for the music to start up.

"Well?"

His ears scarlet with embarrassment, David leaned over the table and hissed between his teeth, "You never found out *when* he died."

"Don't you think so?" Torsson calmly put into his mouth a layered construction of herring, potato, and red onion. But his phlegm did not deceive David. On the contrary, he was afraid that sudden rage would break out again.

"Take it easy," he mumbled nervously.

Yes, indeed, Torsson was horribly calm.

"Oh, so you've come to rap me over the knuckles, have you?" he said. "Really? And you've deduced all that from the interrogation records?"

"You've seen it for yourself," said David, taking a chance. "You kept them in your desk drawer. End of story, you said. But you still had those papers in your drawer."

"I can tell you," said Torsson, "things that aren't in the records. Things only I have heard. When we went to look at him—Matti—they had him in a tool shed. Well . . ." He looked up at David. "I do understand. You were fond of him. Anyhow, that's how it was. He lay in a shed, a kind of shack they had. The person who unlocked the door found it difficult; the key wouldn't turn. They sort of freeze up when they've not been touched for a few days, he said about the key."

"A few days?"

"Aye. Though supposedly I went out there the following day."

"But why didn't you sort that out then?"

"Yes, why? The way things were out there in the dark, you might think the whole thing was imagination, and they were all so unanimous. I'm not particularly good at this sort of thing," he said, suddenly irritated. But he went on all the same. "And the school kids said they hadn't had any craft lessons or art for three days."

"Were those Matti's subjects?"

"Aye. And the adults said he went into town on the Sunday. He died on the Tuesday, in the early hours of Tuesday. Well may you stare at me. But I have to tell you I haven't been all that sure I'd heard right. Not always."

"But you've thought a lot about it."

He felt pity for the large man. Torsson leaned forward with his hand over his eyes.

"I'll say I have," he whispered. "Wait, there's more to come. He went up to the Kaittas tent. Did you read that? Well, he had no lessons that afternoon."

"I read that," said David quickly. "I suppose they usually have Saturday afternoons free?"

Torsson nodded. "You're going too quickly," he complained. "It's taken me months to figure this out."

"Not true. It's taken you months to try to convince yourself you were wrong."

"What shall I do?" Torsson's eyes were childishly trusting.

"Go back to Rakisjokk." David emptied his second drink and went on, his mouth now moving on well-oiled hinges. "You're on holiday. Come with me to Rakisjokk. We'll find out when he died. Nothing else."

Torsson stared at him for a few moments. Then he threw back his head and burst out laughing, a laugh that made one of the Mediterranean musicians blow a false note on his trumpet.

"Ho!" cried Torsson. "You wish! As if I . . ." He laughed again. "Oh, yes, very likely. Here I am, having sat like a rat in a hole for twelve years in this damned darkness. The only time I'm alive is in the summer when I get back home for a while. No, thank you, my lad. You won't get me to Rakisjokk on my holiday."

"You weren't deported here," David mumbled. "You've a will of your own. You can apply for a transfer to that divine Eskilstuna of yours."

Torsson blinked drowsily. "Transfer?"

"You like it here?"

"No!" shouted Torsson with the full force of his lungs.

"You want to be here, all the same."

"Yes," he roared. The air went out of him. "Funny, I've never thought about it. But I do want to be here. If only so that I can go down south in the summer."

"You're an unreflecting man," David remarked in passing. He noticed the drinks had begun to have an effect.

"Let's not talk about it any longer," said Torsson. "That's enough now. I'm going to Eskilstuna early tomorrow morning. I was just being rather sentimental. That lad, this Matti. I didn't know him, but I saw him in that shed. Well."

"Well what?"

"Nothing. He looked so fair and . . . I don't know. Enough of this. Let's eat."

"Fair," David mumbled absently. "I'm glad Matti was fair-haired."

Torsson looked up. "Don't talk rubbish," he said decisively.

"No. I'll re—what's it called?—repay your gratitude. I mean, I'll—"

"You're pissed, man."

"I'll repay your confidence in me," David said quite clearly. "For being allowed to read the records. I'll tell you what I've seen. Do you know what the girl had in that bag?"

"No," said Torsson, yawning.

"A pile of silver ornaments and a cut-through lasso with human hair in it."

He said it as quickly as he could and emptied his glass. He didn't look at Torsson, who was singularly quiet. Then he stumbled on, "Let's drink and be merry. I'm just warning you that I get drunk easily. But don't let's think about Matti. No, not think . . . listen . . . I'll tell you something amusing. Last year in Spain."

David told him about Spain. He did this over the red wine, because that seemed appropriate. With the salt cellar against his plate, he beat flamenco rhythms and clicked imaginary castanets with his right hand in the air. Over his whiskey, he told Torsson about Scotland. He'd never been there, but that mattered less and less. Nor did it matter at all that Torsson had become boring. "Dull old cop," David bawled. He drew a portrait of Torsson on the tablecloth in charcoal. It was very like him, sorrowful pendulous cheeks and eyes looking stern.

"Now I'll transform that banal likeness," David cried ecstatically. "I'll make you human, old copper."

But at that moment the headwaiter grew soundlessly out of the floor in front of them. "I'm sorry, sir."

"What?"

By raising his eyebrows almost to the level of the waiter's, David managed to fix his eyes on the man's face and keep it in his sights so that it swayed no more than insignificantly.

"I'm sorry, but . . ."

The man gestured toward the portrait. He appeared to be looking at a nasty mess of charcoal on a clean linen tablecloth. David leaned toward him. He had put down the charcoal stick.

"I hear you," he said irritably. "I hear you saying you're sorry. You said so before. You say nothing else. Good. You have every reason in the world to be sorry. You look a sorry sight. You look like a depressing grayish yellow —"

"Sir," said the headwaiter severely, straightening up his wavy back.

"Now you're getting a bit of color," said David approvingly. "Pale purple patches on your face."

The waiter closed his mouth quickly, like a perch, then put his hand to his chin.

"Not there," said David. He shook his head and looked at the man through half-closed eyes. "I'm the only one to see them."

"He's an artist," said Torsson in a low voice to the waiter, putting a hand on David's arm.

"Exactly," said David in a loud voice. "Exactly." He was leaning back in his chair, his arms folded, peering at the yellow man with his eyes screwed up. "If I look at you long enough, you'll dissolve," he said, his voice suddenly matter-of-fact and sober.

A trace of a malicious smile played around the corners of the man's mouth as he bowed and retreated.

"What did I tell you?" David intoned. "He's been dissolved. Nothing's impossible for the creative imagination. I created him—a monster. A fragment from a confused nightmare about being in a smoky restaurant. I annihilated him. Now I'm awake again."

He lowered his arms, leaned back in the chair, and fell asleep.

He didn't wake up until five minutes later when the headwaiter arrived with the bill. Torsson had been going to take it and calmly and efficiently see to its redemption.

David's clear blue and wide-awake gaze met his across the table.

"Let me see," he said, snapping his fingers.

Given it, he rapidly checked down the items, the piece of charcoal in his hand.

"Good," he said. "Everything's fine and in order—up to here." He put the charcoal stick against the last item and looked up at the headwaiter's expressionless face.

"Tablecloth, nine kronor," he read.

There was a moment's silence. The man's face still expressed nothing whatsoever, though the right of the two raised eyebrows twitched slightly.

"Now," said David quietly and genially, "now I might get angry." He drew a breath. "Might, I say. Here you have from me a genuine, original, handmade David Malm drawing never before published. And what do you do?"

He allowed the man to swallow.

"You charge me for a tablecloth. I'll say nothing about that. Please observe that I'm not even upset. All I'm saying is that it's quite all right. You're a businessman. You're selling me a tablecloth. You supply the material. You charge nine kronor for it. I say that's all right. I've painted. What I've painted I've painted—"

"Be quiet for a moment and we'll—"

That was Torsson in his caring nursemaid voice.

"Am I getting off the subject? All right. I'll soon be there again. You've sold me a tablecloth. Now I'm coming to you. I'll sell you a drawing."

The headwaiter did something with his mouth that might have become words, but David held up his hand and said solemnly:

"Stop right there. I know what you want to say. You want to make me an offer for it. Unfortunately, you've got

53

it the wrong way around. You put a price on what you sell, and I put a price on what I sell. Right?"

He kept on nodding until he finally got the headwaiter to nod with him.

"So, good. I have a price for the drawing. But all the same, I'll be nice to you. I'll let you guess what I want for a genuine, original, handmade David Malm."

He held the charcoal stick above the bill.

"The guesses are free," he said. "Don't be shy, then all will be well."

The headwaiter pressed a smile out of his lemon-squeezer mouth. "I would guess . . . hm . . . nine kronor. Am I wrong?"

"You're right," said David heartily. "You're a business-man. Born businessman. I congratulate you."

He drew a thick line through the "tablecloth nine kronor" item, subtracted nine from the total and signed the tablecloth.

"You see, I'm not trying to cheat you," he said.

4. TO THE END OF THE WORLD

Seeing a square of blue sky and waking with a terrible hatred in his heart. He certainly wasn't used to this. He must have had her face in his mind's eye in his dream, for now he could see it just as clearly as the starched pleats in the yellow curtain, and he heard her voice, scornful and curious: "Matti's dead."

Without taking his eyes off the window, he knew someone was in the room with him. No sixth sense, just the smell of cheap cigarettes.

"What are you doing here?" he groaned. His head was grinding out its own song of remorse. "Go away. I hate everyone."

He could hear from the breathing that the other man was smiling.

"The boat to Rakisjokk leaves in an hour."

At that, David had to turn over in bed and look at him. Torsson was not in uniform today. He was dressed for his holiday in a Hawaiian shirt and light gray gabardine trousers.

"You're vile," David mumbled. "Wherever did you buy that Christmas wrapping paper you've got around you?" Then he realized what the other man had said. "And when does the train to Eskilstuna leave?"

"It's already left."

David sat up in bed. "Why did you change your mind?"

Torsson knocked the ash off his cigarette and looked thoughtfully at the carpet. "Because Matti Olsson was fair-haired," he said softly.

Then David remembered everything with a jolt that ran like nausea through his body.

"Just to find out *when* he died," Torsson went on tonelessly. "Nothing else."

"You and me," said David, getting his rumpled form out of bed. "You and me. I might die laughing. I don't think we're so well endowed in the brain department."

Torsson's face wore a dogged look.

"I was bottom in everything at school," David mumbled glumly as he filled the basin with water. "I bet she wasn't."

"She?"

"Yes, she. Who else do you imagine will try to stop us?"

He regarded his own round eyes in the mirror and thought they were looking back at him with reproach.

On the jetty at Orjas, Anna Salminen was running around crying alternately, *"Herra jumala* [My God]!" and *"Perkele* [Damn]!" in Finnish. She was giving a hand and advice to Henrik Vuori, who was loading Calor-gas cylinders into the boat. Anna was old and so skinny that she consisted of little more than a hide bag of rattling bones. The flood of tourists during the summer often made her so flustered that she carried on this way.

"Shut up, woman! I wish it was winter soon so you'd come back to your senses," Vuori hissed, heaving a forty-five-kilo cylinder on board.

"Herran tähden, ihminen [For Christ sake]!" Anna whined. Turning around, she froze. She had caught sight of Constable Torsson.

"Have no fear, my good woman," David said. "This wandering work of art with palm trees and moonlight all over him is nonetheless human. He will attack no one."

"He's an artist," Torsson put in mechanically by way of explanation, as had become his habit. Anna transferred her gaze to David.

Henrik Vuori was standing in the boat, staring at Torsson so intently that he forgot to put the fourth and last cylinder in place. The sweat was breaking out on his upper lip with the effort of holding that great weight in his arms.

"Well, now what—"

"Holiday," said Torsson curtly.

"Here? You must have gone off your rocker," Vuori

cried, laughing so hard that the cylinder fell on the deck among the others.

The tourists seated in the boat were looking worried.

"We're off now," said Vuori. "We'll take it carefully." He went over and put the strap around the engine's flywheel and started pulling on it. After the fourth attempt, he looked up at the man sitting nearest to him, a man in full climbing gear, complete with a packet of raisins in his top pocket.

"It's the same with engines as with people," Vuori said. "Free will and the whole caboodle. Now are you going to run or aren't you, you bugger? Must I chuck you overboard?"

David had fallen silent. The long, narrow Rakisjaure had taken his breath away. I haven't got the colors for this, he thought, on the verge of tears.

"Get Anna to shut up, then the engine'll probably run," Vuori mumbled. "It can't stand old women."

Anna replied abusively from the jetty and at that moment the engine started up. Vuori and Anna went on bawling at each other, rudely and heartily. An academic linguist sitting nearby pulled out his pencil and started jotting down Finno-Ugric stems as fast as he could write. Finally, Anna's voice could be heard no more; he gave a deep sigh of satisfaction as he put away his notepad.

They were out on the lake. The wind was brisk and felt strangely snow-cold in the middle of summer. A green cardigan suddenly landed around David's shoulders.

"You're blue in the face," said Torsson. A moment later a scarf followed and he wound it around his ears. As he sat there with nothing but his nose showing—and dripping—he felt someone's eyes on him and turned halfway around.

Of course it was she. The birch-bark knapsack still lay on her lap. He was pleased to note that the white blouse no longer looked clean.

"Oh, so you never got any further?" he hollered. "Thought you were going on down south."

She was silent. Henrik Vuori twisted around and looked at him.

"Had you forgotten your toothbrush after all?"

That little frown appeared again. David grinned and was suddenly scared.

"Shall I throw him overboard for you?" Vuori asked her calmly.

"He knew Matti," the girl said.

Vuori turned right around and looked him up and down. "And the constable's with him?" he said, still joking.

"Niin [That's right]," Torsson replied. *"Mestarisalapoliisi."*

The girl and Vuori exchanged looks. Then Vuori turned to David and said in a friendly voice, "I think he talked about you. You're David, right? A cheerful bloke, he said . . . and kind."

The last word came—he could swear—with a warning note in it and almost a glance at the girl. As if she were something that had to be taken care of.

"No," David shouted over the noise of the engine. "I'm nasty by nature."

"Ho!" Vuori laughed. Torsson patted David's arm to calm him.

Seeing the village in the distance, David kept thinking they'd soon be there. A group of houses lay scattered over the slope below the mountain, with a gray look of poverty about them. He had seen something similar once before, ravaged by the wind and gray with poverty—on the Finnish side of the river Torne. It made no difference that Torsson explained that the people living there were not destitute. It was only the climate that made painting the houses into a labor of Sisyphus. So this was where Matti had lived and had his home. This was the place he had been unable to leave. What use is it to a man, he had said with a smile, if he inherits the whole earth? Vuori turned off the engine and they could hear the rustle of seaweed against the bottom of the boat. Pale fingers curled and swirled under the clear water.

"What's got into you?" Torsson whispered. "You're supposed to be a cheerful bloke."

There were people on the jetty, among them a lithe youth in a red sports shirt, brown-haired and laughing.

"Per-Anti!" Vuori called out. "Look at all these Swedish people I've brought you. They all want lodgings and to go up the mountain."

"Good grief," said Torsson with feeling.

The tourists disembarked onto the creaking jetty. They put on their sunglasses, a sensible idea, because the weary gray of the cottages could be depressing. Now, smiling, they perceived Rakisjokk in various shades of golden yellow. A woman was laughing particularly loudly and happily; she had expensive lenses that let through an exclusive violet light.

Some boys of about fifteen, all Sami and fairly small, their jeans rolled high up their calves, helped Vuori unload the cylinders.

"I've got further education to thank for keeping them here," he said.

At last they had all gone. Torsson sauntered behind Per-Anders Jerf, who had promised him and David a room in his house. Only Vuori was left on the jetty, and David, who had not yet emerged from his paralysis.

"Strange thing about Rakisjokk," he said. "You might think this is where the world comes to an end."

"It does for some people," Vuori replied dryly.

Am I a pathological liar? I enjoy telling lies. At least, I can't stop myself. In heaven's name, what are they staring at? David asked himself as the inhabitants of Rakisjokk scrutinized his face. Torsson and he had been invited to a late dinner at the schoolhouse. Hitherto he had distinguished himself by harping on the one subject.

He improved on it. "We thought it'd be nice to have a bit of a holiday," he said. "The constable and I. Not for the first time, either."

Anna Ryd had not said very much until then, but now she spoke in a clear voice. "But you'd never met until yesterday."

The audience's interest was now so keen and unanimous, they had all inclined their heads to the left. You were guessing, David thought bitterly. But that's no help to me.

"Oh, yeah?" he cried. "So we don't know each other?"

But his voice fell dejectedly at the end and the seven people smiled indulgently, amused. Torsson too was grinning foolishly, which annoyed David, and it occurred to him that they would have smiled that way at Matti, as if at a favorite child. No wiles had been needed to bring him into the conversation. (David had jumped right in out of habit.) No, a great deal about him had reminded them of

61

Matti, and over dinner they had hardly talked about anything else.

He waved his arms over the whitefish in his eagerness to put things right, his ears burning.

"He's lived here for twelve years," he said, jerking his thumb at Torsson, "and every summer he goes off to Eskilstuna and sits there eating almond cakes in the park's outdoor café. I had to come up here to explain to him that this is the place to be in summer."

At that, the stout Torsson straightened up and gave a sigh that made the whitefish sink one level further down through his metabolism. David could see that he was about to speak, and he breathed out with relief. Torsson had authority despite the Hawaiian shirt. He would convince them.

"Well, holiday," he said. "That can wait. But we've really come here to find out when Matti Olsson died."

Flies clumped with ironclad feet across the ceiling during the following seconds.

"Lord, thou canst now let thy servant depart in peace, for his ears have fallen off," said David softly.

Torsson had not emphasized that unfortunate word "when," nor had his voice betrayed a moment's excitement. But the remarkable thing was that no one took up his words. Anna Ryd poked thoughtfully at her fish and didn't even look up.

"Matti was a character," Eklind informed them. He took the deep breath of a public speaker in order to store air for his next words. "His burning artistic soul knew no limitations such as darkness, monotony, isolation."

David stared incredulously at him.

"He turned his back on the city although he could have made a future for himself there."

"Now just a minute . . ." Vuori tapped his fork pensively on the table. "Everyone who comes to the mountain, to stay, I mean, is usually turning their back on something. They all have something they want to get away from."

The whole of Rakisjokk is full of minor Socrates figures, David thought in amazement. But he was beginning to realize that you could say things like that here. Serious, almost sentimental words were still hard currency in Rakisjokk. The words had made such an impression on Erik Sjögren that he put his face in his hands as if praying. David had heard that he had once been an eminent glaciologist. Having come to Rakisjokk to make observations, he had never got away. He looked after the weather, as they said.

"Let's have some coffee," mumbled Kristina Maria Jerf, rising quietly to her feet. "Then you must tell them a story, Henrik."

Smiling, Vuori declined.

"Go on, tell them about the bear."

"Oh, not the bear story! I can't just do that to order. That's like asking Per-Anti to sing a *joik*."

Per-Anders laughed.

"Oh, go on, tell us."

Making a show of reluctance, he started to speak. It was a long, circumstantial story told in stilted phrases that had become set once and for all. David found the slow pace unbearable.

"But why was he angry?" he asked them. "I thought . . ." His voice died away into a silence that showed he had put his foot in it. "I'm sorry, but I don't really understand," he mumbled. "It's like in the Kalevala or something. I'll shut up."

"Safest," Torsson said bitingly.

Oddly enough, Henrik Vuori's story ended with how afraid he'd been when confronted with the bear and how he'd lost his cap by the time he'd managed to get into the boat.

"So the bear got your cap, did he?" said Per-Anders with a laugh, once there was again an opportune moment to speak.

"Aye, he got my cap and put it straight on his furry head. And it suited him. Now he's lolloping around up there with my cap on his head and he walks on his hind legs the whole time, he's become so proud. You've seen him yourself, Per-Anti!"

The Sami solemnly nodded, confirming the statement.

David was not amused. The story was dead boring and sure to be true from beginning to end. He didn't doubt for a second that the bear was stumping around with a cap on its head. Why shouldn't the bears up here be a bit cracked?

"Yeah, well, you're pretty good liars," he said lightly. "Matti said in a letter that, up here, falsehood walks around on two legs carrying the truth under its heart. . . . He found it stimulating, he said. Besides, he didn't say 'falsehood,' he said 'myth,' which sounds grander. He had a feeling for the value of words as well as colors."

At that moment his face went through a transition into scarlet that showed the value of color, and he couldn't understand why. He couldn't even recall what he had said, but sensed that he had made a fool of himself. Not just a fool—he could sense danger. But looking around, he could see nothing but expressionless faces.

Kristina Maria served coffee in the school hall and David found himself at a small table near the door he knew led to the craft room. He sat gazing gloomily at the door, no longer bothering to conceal what had drawn him here. There were so many pitfalls among the marshy tussocks here, there was no point in being careful. But when Torsson sank down on the chair next to his, David nonetheless hissed between his teeth:

"Why did you spoil everything?"

"What?" said Torsson.

"Why did you tell them? Are you stupid?"

"Oh, they're not stupid up here," said Torsson loudly.

David didn't even know whether that was an answer or whether Torsson was hard of hearing. He persuaded himself that Torsson had exaggerated his stories about Rakisjokk. This wasn't a scary place, it was just dull. All he had to worry about was getting through the evening without having to listen to any more bear stories. He jumped up.

"Oh, look, you've got a mah-jongg set! That's a turnup for the books."

Someone laughed quietly.

"Ca-can you play mah-jongg?" The headmaster came hurrying over on his short legs as David got up to take the box down from the shelf.

"Sure I can."

That man irritates me like biscuit crumbs in bed, David thought. Perhaps I ought to warn him.

"Would you like a game?" Eklind asked eagerly.

David slowly pulled out the lid and tipped the box upside down, letting the tiles rattle out over the table. The little headmaster whimpered as if it were his intestines being shaken out.

"Careful, careful!"

"Don't worry," said David. "They won't break. Really nice set. Hand-painted tiles."

"Not of the very highest quality," squeaked Eklind, flattered. "We're going to get a new one. But the importer had none in stock and the ship doesn't arrive from Hong Kong for another three weeks. Do you know what it means, by the way—Hong Kong? Fragrant harbor . . ."

Thirty years ago, Eklind had dreamed of dedicating himself to educating the children of the wilderness, an adventure in howling snow. God knows what he dreamed of now, but he had never succeeded in getting away from Rakisjokk, not even in the summer.

"Oh, Hong Kong?" said David snootily. "Oh, well, that's as good as the ones from Taiwan. But you should try to get a mah-jongg set from the mainland."

"Should we now? You're so well informed . . . Marta and Anna, come on over here. Sit down around the table. Kristina Maria, will you stand down today? You see, it's just us four playing. Go on, sit down."

They did so, looking rather bored.

"Now then, slaves—build the wall!" David commanded loftily, his eyes on Anna Ryd. "And remember, I won't stand for any crooked angles."

Torsson looked interested.

"Can you play?" asked David.

"No, never seen it before."

When his turn came, David took his thirteen tiles from the wall. He had to admit it was a beautiful set. Flowers and seasons glittering with gold, the one of bamboos with its sweeping peacock's tail and gleaming golden eyes.

"How many tiles are there?" Torsson asked.

"Seventy-two with the flowers and seasons," said Eklind swiftly.

"Don't you need them all to play?"

"Oh, yes, all seventy-two."

"But if one's missing?"

"Then the set's spoiled. Just like a pack of cards."

"Huh," said Torsson.

The constable was in his most tedious mood, David thought.

"What's this?" Torsson said. "Why hasn't it got a number on it?"

"Oh, leave it out," David growled.

"It's a dragon, a red dragon," Eklind replied nervously.

"Four of circles," said Anna Ryd, who was the East Wind.

"Why—"

"Oh, be quiet, Torsson. You can't understand this anyway."

"Huh," said Torsson again. But he was greatly intrigued.

"Eight of bamboos."

"Pong."

"Already?"

Marta Vuori didn't reply. Her bony fingers closed around the tile. She laid out the three eights of bamboos face up in front of her and flung a dragon down inside the walls.

"Red dragon. What plans had you in mind?"

"Hey, look at that!" said David, picking up the tile. "Awful!"

"Do you want it?" Marta Vuori asked in a hostile tone.

"No, I just wanted to look at it. It's been spoiled. The colors have run."

"Yes, it's an unfortunate business," said Eklind, his face creasing. "Several tiles have been ruined. They get dirty over time, you know. Now someone's tried to clean them. Unfortunately the paints in this set are water-soluble, so this was the result. None of us did it, and the children aren't allowed to use them. But all the same, I think some of the girls must have been at them. With the best of intentions, of course."

If someone hit you on the head with an iron bar, you'd believe it was done with the best intentions, Torsson thought. And yet David had said he wasn't the reflective kind.

"What are you laughing at, Torsson?"

"Play, don't talk," said Marta Vuori flatly.

"Six of characters."

The game went on. David had managed to scrape up a nice little collection of winds and was beginning to feel the excitement that preceded the realization that he was about to call.

"What the hell's this?" He had taken a tile from the wall and now threw it down. "I've been playing mah-jongg since Grandma was young, but I've never seen anything like that before. What's it supposed to be?"

The tile was white with a green spot carelessly painted in the middle. Nothing else.

"Oh, that's a green dragon," said Eklind apologetically.

"It's not. They look like this." David showed one of his green dragons.

"Let's see," said Torsson.

"You keep your nose out of this."

Marta Vuori laughed, greatly amused by his having revealed that his hand contained a green dragon.

"It's homemade," Eklind stammered. "Made out of a spare tile. One of the green dragons has gone missing."

"Put it down, Torsson. Let's go on. Green dragon. Might just as well get rid of them."

"Mah-jongg," said Marta Vuori.

David kicked open the door of the room Jerf had given them and went straight across to Torsson's bed. He looked at the substantial heap under the covers with distaste.

"I can't imagine why I brought you with me. I simply can't imagine! You spoil everything with your dumb staring and then you go telling them why we're here. And now of course you're asleep, you . . ."

Torsson had the red plaid blanket pulled over his head and did not move.

"Why is the sun shining in the middle of the night? *I* can't sleep. Do something! Think," he went on, pleading. "We'll get nowhere this way. This is for Matti's sake. Oh, you great beer belly, you're just pretending to be asleep!" he yelled suddenly, thumping his fist on the highest point of the bedclothes. The blanket gave way and his hand sank into something soft.

"Yecchh!" cried David.

He spun around. From the darkest corner of the room, where his own bed was, came a quiet sigh. Torsson was sitting on the bed fully dressed, his head on one side.

"That'll do," he said. "That'll do fine. People's imagination will do the rest.

"Now listen. I went to a gym camp when I was twelve. We did this kind of thing then. Apple-pie bed for the games leader. Lads, I'm pissing myself laughing."

Torsson heaved himself off the bed and tightened his belt another notch with a purposeful look. "If it's good enough for you, it's good enough for her."

"Who?"

"She'll only see it from the window, anyway. Come on."

He went ahead of David through the door leading straight outside. The room they had been given was at the back of Jerf's house. Torsson kept fairly close to the cottage wall, then quickly cut across a birch thicket down to the water. It was midnight and the sun was on the back burner, the sea-blue sky reflected into infinity in the water. David walked three steps behind Torsson, watching carefully where he put his feet. The cloudberry flowers had lit a constellation in the marshy ground.

"I'm a person who does his very best," David whispered. "Drop dead with my tongue hanging over the Maginot Line. But I have to know why."

Torsson pressed him down between two birches and took a few steps away to inspect the arrangement.

"Crouch down further," he said. "That's it."

He came closer.

"She'll dump that bark bag," he said. "It was too risky in town. She'll have to sink it to the bottom of the lake. There's a boat over there; I saw her looking at it when she left the school."

"Anna Ryd?"

"No, the Queen of England. Of course. She can't get rid of it in front of the village in this light. It won't get any darker than this tonight. She'll have to make her way out into the bay here. If you lie still here and I do the same over there, then we need only two direction lines . . . those trees on the other side, for instance. Then we can fetch it when she's gone back."

David's mouth had fallen open. "You got that out of a book," he said reproachfully.

"I never read books. Get down now and please don't smoke. I want it," the constable went on, suddenly dreamy, looking out over the smooth water. "The bag."

David could have spent the long wait observing nature, but once Torsson had disappeared into his thicket far out of earshot, he found his field of vision somewhat limited. A few prosaic crowberry clumps stuck up in front of him, the nearest one tickling his nose. A stretch of water, unchangingly smooth and light. A cleared edge of shore on the other side. Four birches, as slender as almond trees in shape. He started thinking about almond trees and then thought, I mustn't fall asleep. Would it really matter if I smoked? But he realized that the smell of pipe smoke would tickle those finely chiseled nostrils and she would turn back.

Since he wasn't wearing his watch, he didn't know how long he'd been curled up with crowberry twigs up his nose. All he could see was the sun sailing eastward, growing smaller and glowing more intensely. The birds dropped off for a few minutes, but now began to whistle again. David's leg had gone to sleep. He moved it with an effort and curled up in a more comfortable position. Had he dozed off?

A sound like silk fabric being ripped apart made him open his eyes wide. Straight ahead of him in his little square of water, splintered rings were swimming on the surface and uneasily absorbing red sunlight. The birchbark bag, he thought. But he could see no boat, nor any living thing on the mirror surface of the water.

The sound came again and now he had time to see the stone cutting through the water and sinking. He knew he was being observed and turned slowly around. The shore behind him sloped up to Jerf's house and he could see the roof gleaming. The slope was empty.

A low laugh could be heard through the anxious twittering of birds. He sat still and the next moment felt a hand on his arm.

"Did I frighten you?"

She was sitting quite close to him in the scrub. Her yellow blouse could be glimpsed through the leaves and she had slipped so quietly through the birches that he'd never even heard her. Or had he been asleep?

"I had to wake you somehow."

He immediately started up his speaking apparatus, thinking he'd start waffling on about bird watching. But the words stuck in his throat. She laughed quietly again, as if she already knew what he was going to say. She got out a pack of cigarettes and offered him one.

"Don't smoke," he said automatically.

"Why not?"

"Er . . . never mind. Birds have no sense of smell, anyway."

She smiled. He didn't like it. She had a cautious upper lip which she drew back over her teeth when she smiled.

"Good," he said. "Just work your charm on me. What do you want?"

"To ask you something."

"Costs nothing."

"You're full of ready-made phrases, aren't you?"

"I have standard formulas . . . thirty-nine B Roman one, alpha—pretty girl asks for something, but she has sharp teeth. Answer: Costs nothing."

"You're here because of Matti?" She ran her forefinger down her straight nose and bit her lower lip.

"I came to see him."

"He's dead."

"I've heard you say that before. Try to sound a bit less pleased about it next time."

Her eyes widened and turned almost black. Oh, no, he thought, that won't work. Not on me. He suddenly felt like squeezing that white throat, where he could see a pulse throbbing restlessly like the heart of a bird. You're the one I'm after, he thought. Why beat about the bush?

"Go back home," she said. "Henrik's morning run leaves at seven o'clock."

He said nothing.

"Go back. Don't try to find out anything more about Matti."

He got up and with a grimace stretched his numb leg. She came after him and put a hand on his arm. It felt cloying.

"Are you listening?"

"Look over there," he said heartlessly. All that could be seen of Torsson, whom he was pointing at, was a generously rounded backside wreathed most reverently in wintergreen and cloudberry blossom.

"Nature doesn't see what expense she goes to," said David. He whistled sharply at Torsson, who lurched up from the undergrowth and stood there looking at them. "Come on!" called David. "I need sleep, all of me except my leg."

While Torsson was approaching, she went on clinging to his arm and talking, her breath hot on his face.

"Stop trying to find out any more. If you were a friend of Matti's. If you really were his friend."

He grasped her hand and held it hard, twisting it.

"What do you want?" he whispered. "Speak out."

"He wasn't what you thought he was. Stop now."

He let go of her hand and she immediately ran off.

5. THE CONSTABLE'S CHINESE SECRET

"I don't mind showing you," Per-Anders Jerf mumbled softly as he unlocked the door of the room. The smell that struck them was musty.

"No, nothing's been moved . . . we somehow don't get around to it. What's the matter with us?"

He was talking to himself. His brown hands drew back the net curtains and he looked at the dust dancing in the ray of sunlight. He put aside a pair of boots standing guard, then ran his hand across the table, which still bore traces of glasses.

"Aye, what are we coming to?" he went on. "There's never enough time and yet time is so long that nothing gets done. This is his room. Oh, dear, those are his trousers hanging there. Think he's coming back, do we?"

Above the sagging couch was one of David's charcoal drawings. "To my friend Matti in the winter." The profile of a Spanish woman shading her eyes in the sun.

"Did you do that?" Torsson asked.

"Uh-huh."

David's throat contracted, and Per-Anders's sorrowful chatter didn't help. This was where Matti had lived in the grayness. This was what he had longed for: a sagging couch with a snuff-brown cover, a scratched table, and a lying mirror.

"Here are all his pictures—all we've done is move the pictures in here from the craft room. Look here—would you believe it?" His bitterness was childish but genuine.

"No," David whispered. "No, but how . . ."

"Aye, that's the way it turned out."

Torsson looked at the pictures Per-Anders held up one by one in the ray of sunlight.

"And this one . . . and this. Do you see? How can you explain it?"

"What is it?" Torsson said sharply. As far as he could see, they were the same pictures he'd seen in the craft room in March. The slashed one was there, too.

"Well, you see . . . he used to be a good painter."

"And?"

"And this . . ." David took the canvas out of Jerf's hands and turned it to the wall.

"Here, look at this!"

He pointed at the wall. A very small portrait of a boy with fair hair hung above the chest of drawers. The boy had a feverish gleam in his eyes.

"He did that one two years ago. What do you think?"

Torsson knew nothing worse than being tested on his nonexistent reactions to art. "Er . . . well, maybe it looks a bit happier."

"No, not happier. But alive. Do you know what this is?"

He pointed to the heap of paintings of marshes and birches which Torsson recognized only too well.

"Apathy. The question is, why did he go on at all?"

"Oh, how can things go so wrong?" Per-Anders mumbled. "Ever since Aili."

"Who?"

"My sister. Only twenty-one." He suddenly looked shy and gazed at his shoes.

"Oh, it was her," said David slowly. "I knew he came to Stockholm for some reason."

"Aye, it was Matti's misfortune that he could never let her go. He went to Stockholm, to art school, when she didn't care about him. And he came back with Anna Ryd. We were all terrified when we saw how like Aili she was. It wasn't good. But Aili just laughed, so softly, so softly," he added, holding out his hands as if his sister were standing in front of him and he wanted to hold her.

"Whatever she may have been thinking," he said, slowly lowering his hands. "But he forgot Anna, whom he'd persuaded to come here and teach. It was as if she had never existed. It can't have been a good time for her, either," he added with naive earnestness.

David had gone over to the chest of drawers and was standing with his back to them.

"And now Aili's dead," he said, no question in his voice.

Per-Anders sucked air through his teeth in an audible yes.

"How do you know that?"

Torsson felt himself distanced, as if David had been to Rakisjokk before him. David turned around quickly and tossed him a photograph that had been standing on the bureau.

"She's very like Anna Ryd. Only her hair is dead straight."

Per-Anders had slumped into a chair. He looked small and old.

"Father will probably never get over it. He lives at Kaittas all the year round now, since she . . . departed. And that's over a year ago. One day he'll fall ill and won't be able to cope up there. But he's determined to stay there. It's as if he believes she's coming back."

"When did it happen?"

"Last summer."

"Did you find her?"

"No. She went up the mountain and didn't come back."

"Why?"

"Oh, why . . . no one knows. Not with Aili. She just laughed."

Silently, Torsson put his hand on David's to stop him.

Per-Anders's voice was very tense. He let out a dry laugh as if to calm them. "It happens," he said.

In the distance, Torsson could hear Vuori's elkhound barking. Suddenly he got the idea that it was dark outside, the snow hurling against the black window. He had to blink in the sunlight to come to his senses.

"It must have been some kind of feast day the day she disappeared," David said in a low, searching voice. "A celebration?"

"Aye," said Jerf, with no surprise. "It was when Marta Vuori came from Kuivakangas to marry Henrik."

"But how do you know that?" Torsson asked.

"Well, she was wearing her best clothes, just like in the photo," said David.

He went over to Torsson and they both looked at the photograph. A slim, dark girl in a wide woolen skirt and the Karesuando Sami women's lace-trimmed cap. With the sun in her eyes, she was peering into the camera and laughing. Her arms were held out as if she wanted everyone to see what fine ornaments she had on: tinkling silver around her belt and neckline.

David looked at the photograph for so long that he thought he could hear the tinkling. "Can you walk four kilometers?" David asked gravely.

"I've never tried."

"Would you like to try?"

Torsson was just as serious. "No."

"But," David said. "There's a but in your eyes."

"But we'd have to take food with us."

"Splendid fat old policeman," said David, moved. "You realize it too. We must go up to old man Jerf. Matti came from there that evening in March. From the old man who's refused to come down and live in the village since his daughter vanished. Presumably he can tell us everything, calmly and quietly."

"Has it ever occurred to you to take her advice?"

"Whose?"

"Anna's. The advice she gave you last night."

"No, it's never occurred to me."

"It's different for me, you see. But you were Matti's friend."

They made preparations. Torsson picked out the route on a map while David spread soft goat's cheese on rye bread. Torsson remarked that it looked sticky. David retorted that things should be sticky on excursions.

"You're supposed to spill juice, sprain ankles, and get ants in your pants. Excursions. Fun."

Before setting off, fairly quietly and without announcing their departure, they rubbed mosquito repellent into their skin. The route to Kaittas ran through the forest. At first they followed the shore of the lake for half a kilometer, losing height all the time. They made their way over the stream on stones and entered the forest where the path was very clearly trampled. The forest was gloomy and monotonous, the trees endless straight ship's masts with melancholy black lichen hanging heavily down. With a whistling sound as if from untuned violins, the mosquitoes went into the attack.

"Interesting," said David, looking at his arms. "I'm going to do this scientifically and I've arranged control groups. I've left certain patches bare. Look, for instance, at this hand. There's no mosquito oil on it. You'd think maybe some mosquitoes would prefer the bare places, others the patches of repellent. But no. The control group on my wrist satisfies its initial hunger and then moves over to my lower arm and enhances its pleasure with the U.S. Army relish. Say what you like about the Americans, but they can certainly make dressings."

"You're painfully amusing," said Torsson. "But I suppose it'll pass."

David wearied somewhat over the next half hour. His voice became whiny as he talked to the mosquitoes about his blood.

"How can you eat that soup?" he asked with pity. "Seventy-three hemoglobins swimming around in a broth that's never boiled with any passion."

Torsson was indifferent to everything except the stitch in his side. Plodding rhythmically along, he remembered once reading in *Reader's Digest* that it came from not exhaling properly. He was listening to the singing blows of an ax striking dry timber. Until now the forest had been silent, with no birds. The blows echoed now quite close, now mockingly distant. Sometimes the ringing sound resounded high up in the mountain. The forest did not thin out; it quite suddenly came to an end. A few tentlike Sami huts lay scattered over the slope in front of them.

Torsson let his rucksack thump to the ground in the dry grass. "Ho!" he yelled.

"And the echo answered—the prophet was silent," said David, after a while.

No sign of life among the tents. The sounds of an ax had ceased in the water-clear air. Acrid smoke was rising into the sky from the smallest of the tents. Torsson went over to it and looked inside. Gutted whitefish were being smoked on a wooden rack in the roof.

"He must live in that big one," said David. "What are you supposed to do? Do you knock or call out, or do you just go in?"

"You look in," said Torsson and did so.

The tent was large and spacious. The fire hadn't gone

out and the smell of smoke was competing against the smell of fresh birch leaves.

"Empty."

"We'll just have to wait."

They dished up coffee on a flat stone and parted the sticky sandwiches. Torsson ate calmly and methodically, his eyes half closed. David was listening all the time for sounds but could hear nothing. The only thing that happened was that a dog appeared on the edge of the forest with a short rope hanging from its collar. They looked at it for a moment. It had a thick black coat and looked thin under its fur.

"Here! Come on, *mustabäna*. . . . *Tjapp!* Come on, boy."

Without a sound, the dog drew back its upper lip and displayed a row of yellow teeth. Then it turned around and disappeared into the forest with the piece of rope dragging behind it.

David fell asleep first, with a handkerchief over his face.

Torsson hallooed for a while at the echo, then stretched out with his rucksack under his head. Shortly afterward, he was snoring trustingly into the blue air.

When David awoke, he was cold. Dark blue shadows were creeping up below the birches and the sun's rays were falling at a more oblique angle. He sat up and looked at the view from which he had fallen asleep. It was like a puzzle in which some pieces had been changed, but exactly which ones he couldn't say. He sniffed the air. The smell of smoke was stronger.

Stiff-legged, he walked over to the little tent where the whitefish was being smoked and looked in. New sticks had been put on the fire. As he wandered over to the big tent with the hearth in it, he sensed he was being observed, but he had no desire to turn around. He stumbled over a bundle of newly chopped sticks in the opening and had a feeling they had been put there on purpose so that he would see them and stumble over them. Was it a practical joke or a warning?

There was no other evidence that someone had been creeping around on soft soles while they slept. He wasn't surprised when he saw Torsson lying on his back in the same position as before, but now with watchful, open eyes.

"I don't like it," he said. "Let's go."

Silently, they collected the remains of their food and, to the delight of the mosquitoes and the manufacturers, covered their arms with another layer of oil.

"Do you feel like giving another shout or two?" said David.

Torsson didn't. They walked quickly through the forest without speaking. After they had gone a few kilometers, they again heard the sound of blows from an ax falling thick and fast.

"And where have you been?"

Marta Vuori's bright eyes were amused. She was standing in the yard in front of the school, a bucket in each hand, on her way toward the kitchen door.

"At Edvin Jerf's, but he wasn't at home," said Torsson before David had a chance to speak.

"And what were *you* going to say, David?" Marta asked, looking at him with her eyes half closed. Her smile had got stuck on her hard lips.

"It's a joy to lie," said David. "I'm a pathological liar."

"By the way, Per-Anders showed us Matti's room and his paintings this morning," Torsson went on methodically. David wondered what he was thinking.

"Per-Anti had a lot to tell you?" Marta licked her lips.

"*Te vaikutatte hermostuneelta,*" said Torsson in a low voice, making David jump up and down beside him.

"Don't do that!" he shouted. "Talk so I can understand!"

Marta Vuori laughed and turned her back on them. The buckets clattered as she vanished through the kitchen door.

"What did you say? Was that Finnish?"

"I just said she seemed nervous."

"That's pathetic. How significant everything sounds in that damned language! Is that just because I don't understand a word? Did you think she looked nervous?"

"No," said Torsson truthfully.

"You know what she'll do now? She'll go straight to Per-Anders, twist his arm, and tell him not to speak to us."

"Do you think so?"

"Not really," said David feebly. "I don't know anything. But I'm going to learn a rude word in Finnish, a really offensive one, and every time you speak Finnish, I'll say it over and over again until you're embarrassed."

He looked at Torsson, only to see he wasn't listening.

"Don't be childish, David, said he wearily. . . . Let's go in and take an after-dinner nap, Torsson."

Between one and five, the prevailing state in Rakisjokk was something like a siesta. Vuori's long motorboat, the *Hork,* had gone back with the morning tourists and would not be returning to the jetty with those who were to stop overnight until five o'clock. The party guided by

Per-Anders was winding its way up the friendliest slope of the mountain, and looked no bigger than a column of greenfly. Vuori's dog was lying on the jetty, nose between its paws, sleeping, slobbering, and waiting.

David and Torsson went into their room, eyes blinded by the light. After blinking a few times, they saw that Erik Sjögren was sitting on David's bed, his smelly pipe crackling. He looked as if he'd been waiting a long time.

"Where've you been?"

"We can't complain of lack of interest in us," said David.

"What are you looking for?"

Torsson saw he was dressed just as he had been last winter, in gray trousers and an Icelandic sweater. He wondered whether Sjögren ever changed his clothes.

"We've already told you," said Torsson in an unexpectedly thin voice.

"You scare me," said Sjögren, grinning. "What old stories are you going to drag up? Are you sure I've been cleared of that Matti business?"

"Aye," said Torsson. "Of course."

"The doctor established that he had frozen to death . . . the blow wasn't fatal. Isn't that right? And the blood came from his hand. He'd cut his hand."

Erik Sjögren had long ago stopped talking about Matti except as a corpse. None of the others appeared to have forgotten the living Matti so quickly. But the dead Matti filled him with a childish terror.

"Why don't you leave?"

He reminded David of a child at the doctor's yelling "Time to go now" the moment he got in through the door. Where will you run to next time? David thought. You can hardly go farther away than here. But you must have some kind of destiny, you poor bastard. He suddenly hated him for talking about Matti as a problem, a personal danger.

"Stop gibbering," he burst out. "Tell us when Matti died instead. What have you all been cooking up? What is it that makes you all get together and lie?"

Sjögren got up and took his pipe out of his mouth. "Lie?" he said. "I don't understand."

"You can do better than that," said David. "Try again."

The visitor left them with a furtive look, as if he had found himself in bad company.

"You went a bit over the top," said Torsson as the door slammed. "Cool it."

"But he knows they're lying."

"He knows nothing. He's forgotten everything except that he's frightened."

An air of disapproval manifested itself toward the evening. No one asked them to drop by. They were being frozen out and, not used to unkind treatment, David took his invented errands from house to house.

"I'll stop wagging my tail now," he announced at about nine o'clock and parked himself for good on his bed with the table pulled up in front of him. The sound of laughter and singing from the schoolhouse did not make things any better.

" 'Red-painted cottages,' tum tum tum ta . . . That Eklind really has managed to preserve a touch of the seminary over the years. What about a riddle, Torsson?"

"Mmm," Torsson growled over a three-day-old evening paper.

"I could solve this in my sleep: a word game and what politicians do for votes."

"What?"

"Scrabble."

"Babble you certainly can, even in your sleep."

"That's cheap, Torsson."

A whiff of turpentine was rising from the table.

"What are you doing?"

"I'm cleaning the mah-jongg tiles that got spoilt. I thought I'd repaint them for Eklind. I've a few small brushes left from my naturalistic period."

Torsson was fascinated by David's hands, seeing them purposeful for the first time, moving rapidly and adroitly over his work. He started arranging paints on the palette, squeezing tubes and letting the oily paint run out in glistening snakes.

"Surely you don't need that much?" said Torsson, a careful man.

"It's fun."

"Won't it be terribly finicky work? With so many colors on each of them. I don't suppose you've got gold?"

"No, I've never had any kind of oriental period. I'm entering one now. I shall paint you like Omar Pasha with gold on your eyelids and fat slave women bearing veal steaks and peacocks' eyes. As a matter of fact it won't be too finicky because I'm in luck. Only dragons are damaged and they have only one color each."

"Why is that?" Torsson put down his paper.

"I seem to have heard that question before. Why? It's perfectly obvious. Whoever washed these tiles started with the dragons because they have the largest area of white and so look the dirtiest."

"Oh, I see. I thought it was—what's it called?—a mah-jongg hand."

"Not at all. There are only four tiles. You need fourteen to go mah-jongg."

"Then I was wrong."

For some reason he looked unhappy.

"What have you gone and thought up now?"

"Listen to them."

They listened in the direction of the schoolyard.

" 'The flowers of the fo-o-o-rest . . .' Why aren't we invited? That knife-sharp soprano must be Anna Ryd."

"No, it's not. She's got a fairly deep voice. It's one of the schoolgirls. They've gathered all the children there."

"Open fire, roasted apples, and guessing games. It's like on television — the Gösta Eklind show."

David had begun to insert paint into the depressions forming the character of the dragon, the tip of his tongue following snakelike the delicate movements of the brush. The job took a long time and Torsson watched without taking his eyes off the tip of the brush. When he had finished, David carefully put the tiles in rows of three — the red dragons with their sharp swordlike character and below them the green dragons with their finely curved character.

"Why are you putting them like that?"

"They have to dry."

"Yes, but why just like that?"

"I wasn't thinking. Out of habit, I suppose. Beginning a mah-jongg hand. Do you know what I'd get?" He stared in fascination at the tiles. "If I had the white dragons. And another green one . . . but the green dragon's gone missing, of course."

"What would you get?"

"I'd go mah-jongg."

"But you need fourteen tiles for that."

"Not for this special hand. It's a limit hand. All you need is three white, three red, and two green."

"Dragons?"

"Yes."

Torsson drew a deep, quavering breath and leaned back in his chair. "What do the white dragons look like?"

"They're just white. No coloring on them. No character."

"So if you washed them, it wouldn't show?"

"No, not at all."

"Get them out."

David rummaged in the box for the white dragons. He put them in a neat pong above the red ones and looked at them.

"How clean they are," he said.

"Indeed."

In the silence they could hear footsteps on the gravel in the yard. David looked out of the window.

"It's Eklind," he said. "The headmaster has relented. We're to be invited to community singing and carbonized apples."

Eklind had a way of coming through doorways that made those inside nervous. His head came in first like a cautious bird's, then a foot in a black boot poked through the crack.

"Am I disturbing you?"

"Not at all."

He went over to the table and looked at the tiles, his hands clasped over his stomach, his bushy hair moving faintly in the draft from the door.

"How nice of you," he said. "How very kind. You

really must be a true mah-jongg enthusiast. May I congratulate you, by the way?"

"What on?"

He laughed and tugged at the knot of his tie. "You're on your way to going mah-jongg—one of the limit hands, of course, as you haven't got fourteen tiles."

"No," said David, "I haven't. And we're not playing, either."

Torsson cleared his throat and looked embarrassed. When he opened his mouth, he turned slightly red.

"Hrrm . . . can't one say David's—um, er . . ."

"Calling. Of course. He only needs one tile."

Torsson had taken out a tobacco pouch—David had never seen him smoking anything but cigarettes before—and was digging into the dry crumbs of shag. Getting out a little packet of typing paper carefully sealed with tape, he levered up the strips of tape with his fat fingers. Eklind followed his activities with the irritation one clumsy person always experiences faced with another. Finally Torsson had freed his treasure and placed it on the table beside the green dragon.

"Mah-jongg," he said.

Eklind laughed. "Why, that's our tile! Our missing green dragon. But look at the state of it! What are those brown spots?" He held out his hand.

"I don't want you to touch it," said Torsson calmly.

Eklind drew back his hand. "Eh?"

It had begun to dawn on him that the atmosphere in the bright, hot little room was unpleasant. He glanced in confusion at David but was given no help. David was looking at the tile and the brown spots, then up at Eklind as if waiting for something.

"I'm pretty stupid at mah-jongg and that kind of thing," said Torsson. "I don't know the rules. But isn't this . . . this hand . . . Big Three Dragons?"

"Yes," said Eklind. "Of course. How extraordinarily amusing."

"Do you think so?" said Torsson.

6. SACRIFICE IN RAKISJOKK

That night David woke from a dream in which a door was slamming. When he sat up in bed, wide awake, the echo of the slam was rolling down the mountainsides. It sounded as if the echo had lungs that constantly filled with new air; it lasted a long while before it died away on a singing note.

"What was that?"

Torsson was awake and had got out of bed. It looked

like being a cloudy day and the light coming through the window was dawn-sharp. He picked up his watch from the bedside table and looked at it.

"Four," he said.

A moment later a second shot rang out. This time they could hear clearly that it was a shot, but once the echo took over and hurled the sound between the mountain walls, it stopped being real. A bird whistled warningly from the lake, but that was a violin note from a Stravinsky opera and just as unreal. Torsson was about to pull on his trousers and rush out.

"*Was* that a shot?" said David.

Afterward he couldn't swear to it any longer. Torsson had his head on one side and was listening. But it was quiet now, acres of silent wilderness holding their breath. The morning chill lay defiantly in wait for anyone wishing to set foot on the wet grass.

Later, they blamed their dazed state for the fact that they got away so late. Torsson was convinced the sound had come from up the mountain. The houses maintained their morning silence with their gleaming rectangles of black windows. As they passed the back of the school-house, David jumped when the row of buttons on his open jacket struck an empty Calorgas cylinder with a dry echo. Jog-trotting, they made their way through the birch thickets up a steep ascent, in passing breaking off leafy branches with which to ward off the mosquitoes, whose tuneless war song buzzed in their ears.

"Where are we going?"

Torsson didn't know. He was trudging along, going by his recollection of the echo, hoping they would find their way. With every step he had to slacken his pace because his breath was making his throat sting. The birches thinned out, and he suddenly heard a sucking noise as he pulled his foot out of a tussock. They had come out on the marsh.

A faint, icy wind, barely touching their cheeks, predicted steady drizzle, and it was soon pouring coldly down on them in the gray silence. A smell of decay rose from the squelching ground. Here and there the water glinted darkly. David's teeth were chattering and he was shivering in his soaking-wet jacket. The ground beneath his feet felt alive, or no more than half dead. It kept moving slowly away from him, sucking sleepily at his legs.

"We must get out of here."

He leaped away in panic toward the birches.

"Take it easy, or you'll get stuck."

David left a shoe behind him in a black hole but didn't turn around until he had firm ground under his feet. Torsson came trotting after him and put a cigarette into his mouth. He was carrying the missing shoe, now dripping on the end of a stick.

They ascended through the birch forest again, found a path, and followed it. The rain came creeping toward them in glittering rivulets off the slope. They startled a large bird whose flapping wings made a noise like gunshot when it took off. Soon after that they heard two real shots, distinct and definite.

"Four," said David.

Now they knew in which direction to go. The path pointed that way.

"Four," Torsson repeated without expression. "He ought to have scored a hit by now."

David suddenly realized what might have happened. He wanted to turn back. Did he really want to see what they were searching for? But Torsson was ahead now. His breathing was sharp and gasping, but he didn't slacken his pace. They didn't know how long they'd been walking. All they knew was that the rain had stopped and the air was turning chilly from the height. The birches were smaller now and thinning out, daylight over the mountain showing a confusion of stonecrop in colors ranging between rust and bile yellow.

They couldn't keep up that pace forever on the steep rise. Torsson sat down on a stone in the shelter of some undergrowth and David crouched down beside him. They lit pipe and cigarette and didn't speak. A minute or two later, David shushed his companion. At first they could hear nothing and thought he was mistaken. But then there was no mistaking the sound of soft springy footsteps on the ground. Someone was coming toward them down the path.

The footsteps were right on top of them before they got around to making themselves known. Was there any chance they might not be seen? Crouching down further was no use.

Still no one came in sight. Then David raised his head above the undergrowth. They both stared, riveted, at the barrel of a rifle bouncing in time with the steps just above the flags of green birch leaves snapping in the wind.

"Stop! *Muuten ammumme* [Or we'll shoot]!"

Torsson licked his lips. But the footsteps stopped at the sound of his voice. Then there was a sound, something halfway between a sob and a laugh.

"What with?"

David sighed, realizing they were both visible through the leaves from where the bearer of the rifle was.

"What are you planning to shoot with? David's pipe?"

The rifle clattered down at their feet. He had thrown it.

The next moment he pushed aside the branches and stood in front of them. David realized that what he had heard was more of a sob.

Per-Anders Jerf was wearing a vest and tight, stained, woolen trousers. His shoes weren't laced and his hair was disheveled. He had blood on his hands far up above his wrists, and David's stomach turned slowly over. Jerf had wiped tears and grime off his face until it too was blood-stained. He was twisting a red woolen scarf in his hands. Suddenly he threw that, too, then flung down his sheath knife. David grimaced. It had been used.

"What's going on?" asked Torsson, slowly getting up. His movements were guarded.

"Come and take a look," said Per-Anders. "Bring the rifle, Torsson, if you're afraid of me."

He started walking ahead of them along the path, which became less distinct on the bare ground. Then he suddenly changed direction and started climbing up a rock face with long, agile movements. They had to keep up as best they could; he didn't look back. After a while they found themselves standing on a windy plateau. Large patches of dirty, grainy snow remained in the shady spots. Two bodies were lying outstretched on one of the patches of snow.

Per-Anders went across and started cleaning his hands with snow, which was so sharp and coarse that he made a face.

"They're timid," he said. "They would have gone off long ago if they hadn't been dead. Look at my poor reindeer . . ."

He took hold of one of the reindeer heads by the antlers and swung it around until a blank eye met David's gaze.

"What happened?"

"Didn't you hear the shots?"

"Aye. That's why we came out. Was it you shooting?"

"Aye, the last two."

"And the others?"

"They woke me. But whoever was shooting didn't do a proper job. When I got up here and found the reindeer, one was only injured but couldn't get away. I was shaking so hard that it took me two shots to kill it."

He showed his hands.

"I had to use the knife so that they wouldn't go to waste. Well, I've taken part in reindeer slaughter many a time," he said, then started desperately rubbing his hands with snow again.

"And you took the rifle with you?"

"No."

"Isn't it yours?"

"Yes, it's mine. But it wasn't there when I set off. It was up here with the barrel stuck in that hole there."

He showed them a crack in the mountain that had been stuffed with moss.

"And so that I'd know just where it was when I came to fetch it, this red scarf was tied around the butt."

He sank to the ground, his legs tucked beneath him. With trembling hands he started to dig his pipe and tobacco out of his trouser pockets. When he went on, his voice was low and steady.

"And so that I'd be sure to know what I was up against, it was Matti's red scarf around the rifle." The last two shots had definitely woken Rakisjokk. It had gone six by the time they got back down there, and people were still standing shivering in the morning chill outside the school. Anna Ryd had thrown a shawl over her nightdress and she pulled it closer around her when she caught sight of David. Per-Anders stopped on the path just above the school and looked down at the crowd of people. His upper lip curled back over his narrow teeth.

"Oh, so you're back home already, are you?" he shouted.

His voice produced a single short echo up in the mountain. Silence fell again, as if the gray cottonwool sky had absorbed the sound. David pulled Jerf's arm to get him to go with them down to the yard, but he wouldn't move.

"You think I tell David and his policeman too much. Are you afraid I'll tell them everything?"

"What's happened?" Kristina Maria, down in the yard, demanded to know.

"Two reindeer have been shot," he replied. "And don't think I didn't get that fine hint. But the thing about me is"—he shifted his feet in the slippery grass as if wanting to assure himself he was standing firm—"that I don't let anything scare me. On the contrary. If it weren't for the reindeer you've shot, maybe I wouldn't have told the police anything, but now I'm going to. Now I'm about to walk between these two into my house and tell them, and there's nothing you can do about it. You were a fool to take my gun. Don't we know each other better than that up here? You should've known you can't scare me into keeping my mouth shut."

He took a firm hold on David's arm and started off down the path. They passed quite close to the silent group in the schoolyard. Eklind alone stammered something as they walked past.

"But who?" David asked as soon as they were behind Jerf's shed and on their way up to his house.

"Who what?"

"Who were you talking to?"

"I don't know."

"You don't know?"

"No," he snapped. "I don't know which of them it is. But one of them must know what I'm talking about."

He went straight into the kitchen and filled the soot-blackened coffee kettle with water from the bucket. He jammed birch bark and paper into the stove, getting a fire going faster than David could light his pipe. As the kettle began to hiss, he stood over the washing bowl, scrubbing the blood and dirt off his hands. Kristina Maria had slipped into the kitchen while he had his face in the water, huffing and snorting so he didn't hear her. Then her skirt swept around his legs and he raised his head and stared at her, soapy water trickling past his eyes.

"Get out!" he hissed, a raised vein throbbing at his temple.

Kristina Maria didn't move.

"Go on, Ristin," he repeated, his eyes narrowing.

Kristina Maria mumbled something in Sami and disappeared out into the cold morning, a water bucket rattling at her side.

David had got the impression that Per-Anders was a sensitive young man to whom tears and sad words came easily. Despite his palpable rage, that impression remained. A sob always seemed to be lying in wait in Per-Anders's throat, and without drawing breath, he swore lengthily in Sami to suppress it. Once he had filled their cups with coffee, strong and steaming, he dumped bread and soft goat's cheese on the table in front of them, then sat down on the chair with his feet tucked in.

"Listen and I'll tell you," he said. "The truth is that Matti didn't die on the Monday night. By then he'd already been dead for three days. He died on the Saturday, or in the small hours of Sunday morning."

David noticed Torsson buttering a slice of bread without looking up.

"It's not so easy for the doctors, either," Per-Anders went on. "He was in that shed a long time before being taken to town, and he was frozen through. But that's how it was, and now it's been said."

"That's not enough," said Torsson.

Jerf was silent and drained his cup.

"That doesn't tell us anything about why you all decided to lie to us."

For the first time Per-Anders seemed to realize what he had let himself in for.

"You see," he mumbled, "we had to. Because we didn't find him. We were ashamed we hadn't missed him earlier."

"Per-Anti, why did you take half an hour to come up to the school the morning you found him?" Torsson asked gently.

Per-Anders's eyes narrowed. "I was going up to look for reindeer. I took the track behind—"

" 'Miksi sinä niin sanot? Pidähän varasi!' "

"You heard her."

"Yes. Your sister warned you when you were about to tell me. 'Why did you say that? Watch out!' she said."

"Niin [Aye]. But how did you figure that?"

"You said you left home before eight. Anna Ryd hurried across the schoolyard to be in time for a lesson at half past eight. There's a gap. I think you got farther than the schoolyard in that time."

"You seem to remember everything."

"Let's go," said Torsson, suddenly cheerful. "Lähdemmekö? Show me the place where you found him."

"What is it?" asked David. "What are we going to do?"

"Now you've been so good and quiet for a long time, please keep your mouth shut for a little bit longer. Come on."

They crossed the schoolyard without seeing a soul. The air had grown warmer and there was a glimpse of the sun. David had still not changed his clothes, having nothing to change into, and he felt cold in his wet jacket.

"We'll walk exactly the same way I went that morning," said Jerf. "Though I was on skis."

"Which morning was it?"

"Tuesday morning. He'd been missing since Saturday evening. But he'd talked so much about going to town on Saturday night, and a pair of skis had gone, so we didn't give him much thought—well, we did, but we expected to hear from him. I took the path here . . . we have a ski track following the path in winter. I was going up to my reindeer."

It didn't take half an hour to get there, nor even half that time. But Per-Anders explained that he had stood beside Matti's body for a long time.

"This is where he was lying."

A birch bowed gracefully over the place where he had lain.

"The skis lay beside him. He looked as if he was sleeping, but quite a lot of snow had covered him."

Per-Anders sank to the ground and pulled his feet under him.

"I went straight back to the school, where I ran into Anna. She went off up there, running in the deep snow, while I went for the sled. When I got back there, she was lying over Matti's body, weeping—no, wailing."

David grimaced. "Method or melodrama?"

"I don't understand."

"Doesn't matter."

"Well, what else is there to tell you? We went back. I had him in the sledge and she used his skis. Well, the skis were actually matron's, he'd borrowed them. They were kept behind the school, by the craftroom door. He probably took the first pair that came to hand. So they fitted Anna well."

"Hold it," said Torsson. "There was something . . ."

"What?"

"I don't know."

His concentrated expression gradually changed into a foolish grin. "Then Matti must have had small feet," he said.

"Not particularly."

"But the skis? Of course, he must have adjusted the bindings."

"Aye."

"So she adjusted them back?"

"She did what?"

Torsson shook his head. "Go on," he said. "Why did you all agree to say he died on the night between Monday and Tuesday?"

"Well, we thought we ought to have gone to look for him. But, see, he'd said he was going into town. The school would get a bad reputation . . . we might even be held responsible. I can't think where we got this notion, but in the winter darkness, anything's possible up here." He hunched his shoulders, shrinking into his seat.

"Erik was terribly frightened, too."

"Was it Sjögren who thought it all up?"

"No, I don't think so. It was all of us."

"Oh, no," said Torsson sharply. "One person has an

idea and persuades the others. Then it just looks as if everyone has thought the same thing."

"I don't know." Jerf shook his head glumly.

"But if you knew who it was, then you'd know who shot your reindeer."

Per-Anders looked up. "I'll find that out," he said, and his soft voice carried menace.

"But the rest," said Torsson, "about the party? Was that true?"

"All the rest is true, though it happened on the Saturday. But otherwise it's all true. So I don't know whether it changes anything."

They started off down the path again. The roof of the school appeared, a thin spiral of smoke rising from its chimney. Now long past seven, there should have been some life in the village, but people stayed indoors. The *Hork* had left the jetty. They could hear its engine chugging out on the lake, then suddenly stop.

"Dirt in the carburetor," said Per-Anders.

"Free will."

David listened for the coughing sound of it starting up again. The silence around them was made oppressive by the sound. There was an atmosphere like a hangover. Lack of sleep was making their eyes smart; the fear and excitement had subsided and settled in their legs.

"I suppose I must get some help and go up to see my reindeer," said Per-Anders, wearily rubbing his eyes. He started walking faster and had soon drawn ahead of them, keeping to the side of the path all the time as if afraid to leave the shade of the birches.

"We were in luck," said Torsson. "Lucky we went up there. If we'd met him now, we'd never have got anything out of him."

"Why not?"

"He's becoming frightened."

When they got back to the house, they flopped down on their beds and David felt as if he would fall asleep immediately. The mah-jongg hand was still lying on the table, giving off a faint whiff of turpentine. The oil paint gleamed prettily in the grooves. David lay listening for sounds. He heard buckets striking against each other and quick steps on the gravel. Out on the gray water, the coughing of the *Hork* grew fainter. He didn't sleep. Toward the afternoon, David took his sketchbook and charcoal and went up on the hill behind Jerf's house. A pattern in the birches interested him — a parade of gently bowing arches repeating itself and fading away toward the marsh. Torsson had half gone back on duty and was busy finding out who had shot Per-Anders's reindeer, but he seemed to be doing it with the help of the *Reader's Digest*.

Because of the sun — back to high-summer strength again, clouds gathering on the horizon — David had borrowed a cap. It was Per-Anders's Sunday-best Sami cap with a pompon the size of a child's head. He pulled it down over his ears and crouched down on the ground with his legs beneath him, his sketchbook propped up against a large stone.

"Have you seen our new native artist? A new Nils Nilsson Skum?"

Henrik Vuori had come by with a group of tourists and they stopped at a respectful distance.

"*Jumalan terve,*" whispered David piously. He had begun to learn a thing or two.

"What did he say? Was it in Sami?"

"No, Finnish. It means 'Peace be with you.' "

"They say their art still has a magical-ritualistic significance," a gentleman in a plastic raincoat pontificated, and his wife took a snapshot of David. David held out his hand and snapped his fingers.

"He wants money," said the wife with a gasp. "Göran, have you got any change?"

"Five kronor—me sing *joik*," David mumbled into his cap.

"Are you sure he's a *real* one? A real Sami, I mean."

"He's real enough," said Vuori calmly. "Per-Anti, look at your brother!"

Per-Anders walked over from his shed, and for the first time that day, David saw him smile.

"Me real. Tasty ethnographical morsel," said David happily.

The man in the plastic raincoat snorted and the company went on with Vuori laughing quietly in the lead.

"That was a joke in poor taste." The voice behind David was sharp and familiar. "You're not exactly furthering the Sami cause by carrying on like that."

"Oh, come on, Anna. No harm in a bit of fun," said Per-Anders, glancing at her. Her dark hair was scraped back more severely than ever. Her outline had something in common with the birches, and but for his hatred, David would have drawn it in charcoal.

"Oh, so you haven't left yet?" David said.

"Left?"

"When we met, you said you were going 'a long, long way away.' That's not wishful thinking on my part. You promised to do me that favor."

She didn't reply. Her slim foot fidgeted in the grass and Jerf stared at it. Suddenly, Per-Anders leaned down and grasped her ankle. Anna teetered on one leg, then most ungracefully sat down in the grass.

"What are you doing?"

"What small feet you have!"

"Let me go, Per-Anti. You're hurting me."

Her voice remained controlled and deliberate. Per-Anders let go of her foot and stood up.

"You never adjusted the bindings."

"What are you talking about?"

She brushed the grass off her skirt, her lips pressed together.

"Don't you remember? That morning we found Matti? You took matron's skis from where they were lying beside him, and you skied down to the school. I can see you now, just as that morning. You put the skis on in a second."

That threw her. Nervously, she tucked a strand of hair behind her ear. David had put down the sketchbook and was listening open-mouthed.

"Matti never had those skis on!" Per-Anders shouted.

"Never had . . . I don't understand."

Slowly she began to retreat backward, still fiddling with recalcitrant strands of hair.

"Such a fatal little mistake in all that self-control," said David softly. "How could you?"

"I . . . ?"

She flung out her hands, then turned quickly around and ran from them, stumbling in the slippery grass. Per-Anders went after her with short, springy steps. He had already gone when Torsson appeared.

"What's all the shouting about?"

David told him.

"Oh, I knew that."

"That means he never went up there on skis?"

"How do I know what it means?"

"But how did he get there?"

"I don't know. It had snowed, after all. But if it hadn't snowed, perhaps Per-Anti would have seen something." He looked up, thinking, his mouth half open. "Hey, look at him."

Jerf was rather wearily coming back across the yard.

"Wonder what a couple of reindeer cost?" said Torsson.

"What are you thinking of now?" asked David. "He's told us everything. About Matti and the Saturday evening and all."

"Well, sooner or later we would have found out anyway. Do you think he'd sacrifice a couple of reindeer to get us on his side?"

7 . DAY OF WRATH

Gösta Eklind, the headmaster, has not yet managed to rise to the rank of the most important person in this story. But he is certainly the most well-meaning, though he has made a mistake inviting his entire circle of acquaintances, including the policeman and his hanger-on David, to coffee on the lawn outside his small house.

"My dear Per-Anti," he says, with attentive servility, "have some Swiss roll."

This is his concession to the two reindeer skins now hanging in a cloud of flies on the wall of the shed. With the best of intentions, Eklind has brought out his checkbook and offered Per-Anders a handout. But Jerf, who is not poor, bared his teeth in a mordant grin.

The echo of the early morning shots is still throbbing against their eardrums; all topics of conversation soon dry up. Everyone wants to get to the point. But how to explain, without attracting attention thereby, that you're nearsighted and have never touched a rifle? Even Kristina Maria would like to explain, and yet she owns the reindeer jointly with her brother. She's begun to fear his fierce, searching look.

Yet it is Kristina Maria, the quickest thinker, who finally lets them all off the hook.

"Shame that Henrik has to take his boat out every day! He should have been here."

The coughing of the *Hork* has long since died away across the water, and a liberating sense of security settles over the company. Henrik has never before had so much praise heaped on him. Not that anyone directly states what an excellent shot he is, but why shouldn't Kristina Maria tell them about that time when he crept up on a whole herd of summer reindeer without their catching his scent? They were rolling around in the patches of snow to freeze the horsefly eggs . . .

That's right, patches of snow. The words are out.

But Marta Vuori has come out of the school with fresh coffee at the very moment Kristina is praising Henrik to the skies, and David cringes. For Marta is as determined as a Wagnerian Valkyrie and is carrying the coffee like a dedicated sword in front of her. For a moment she stops in front of Kristina Maria as if having second thoughts. Then she lowers the coffee kettle and starts with her cup, and without raising the spout, she continues on to the next cup in a sweeping brown flow of coffee. She does two whole rounds and then says, "There you are."

"Thank you," whispers Eklind, his lips trembling. Thus his little party is ended and his fine white tablecloth is soaked in a brown circle with wasps buzzing around it.

Kristina has been sitting over her coffee, her eyes gritty with sleeplessness. She has had an uneasy night and her anxiety began hours before Rakisjokk heard those shots. Two hours after midnight she was still awake, as so often on these light nights. She slept in the kitchen and was lying there looking longingly at the coffee kettle when she heard footsteps on the gravel outside. Why should she concern herself with footsteps? People were often out and about in the summer night. The sun made folk restless, and they could always sleep in the winter.

But these were such cautious footsteps. Someone was putting down first one foot, then the other, pausing to listen in the stillness. Kristina Maria scrambled out of her bench bed and put her feet down on the cold floor. She was smiling. How about surprising that fat policeman on his nighttime prowl?

She threw an old raincoat over her shoulders and went out of the kitchen. The rifle barrel gleamed coldly on the wall by the front door—she would particularly remember that. No one bothered to lock doors in Rakisjokk, and she only had to touch the handle to make the door swing open. The night air enveloped her. At first she thought there were figures moving about everywhere, but that may have been just the wind letting odd shadows cast by birches fumble over the houses. The slightest rustle of gravel soon betrayed the person standing in the shadow of Per-Anders's shed, one foot poised for a cautious step.

Kristina Maria reckoned this was all rather silly. She had once been to the Royal Opera in Stockholm and the people in the opera had crept around in a peculiar way, mixed each other up, and kept appearing in dark corners. But the difference was that on the stage there had been deep shadows to hide in between the pools of light from the spotlights. Here the eternal light prevailed, drab and tormenting at this time of night. Time seemed to stand still in this light, pressing against your temples. Oh, winter, please come. . . .

What was she thinking? Her lips felt stiff as she mumbled the words, looking around for some wood to touch.

"What are you doing here?"

She spoke quietly in Swedish. She could clearly see that it was Anna Ryd standing there in the shadow, curiously got up in an old coat. The gray of the coat was probably intended to blend into the night air, but the white edge of her nightdress below the hem gave her away. Anna gave a short laugh.

"Nothing."

"Well, then, go back to bed," she muttered.

"No."

"Can't you sleep either?"

"No."

"It's the light."

She couldn't see Anna's face all that well, but she noticed her feet impatiently shuffling. Kristina Maria did not easily lose her patience. Until she was seven, her father had been on the move with the reindeer and then life had been mostly waiting. She had waited for hours in pouring rain for the roundup to get under way. Waited for reeking damp firewood to catch, for dogs that had run away.

"Well, I suppose we'd better go back to bed."

"You go on."

Kristina Maria sounded slightly scornful. She badly wanted to know why Anna didn't move. Smiling, she leaned against the doorpost.

Anna started walking. But—Kristina Maria leaned over to follow her movements—she was walking backward. In four or five steps she was level with the shed wall, then made a strange twist with her body and vanished behind the shed. Now she could be heard running, no longer cautious.

Once she had crept back into bed, it took Kristina Maria a long time to work out why Anna had behaved like that. When she was half asleep, the answer came to her. Anna had been carrying something on her back that she did not want anyone to see.

Kristina Maria doesn't take her eyes off Anna today. As long as she stays in her room, she is left in peace, but as soon as she shows herself in the yard, those brown eyes are on her. Kristina Maria hasn't said a word to the others about what happened last night. No mention of how close Anna had been to the rifle on Per-Anders's wall. That frightens Anna more than anything else, Kristina Maria's ability just to wait and observe without confiding in anyone.

After coffee with the headmaster, Kristina Maria gets quickly up from the grass as soon as Anna has disappeared around the corner of the cottage. But Eklind stops her for a moment—he's behaving over those two reindeer as if there's been a death in the family. She doesn't catch sight of Anna until she's far down by the shore. It is not clear whether Anna has anything special to do there. She's walking at random and Kristina Maria has to stop behind the brewhouse to escape a hasty glance over Anna's shoulder. She stands between clumps of tall willow herb, absently crumbling the flowers in her fingers and letting them fall to the ground. When she's sure Anna has a good start, she takes a step out.

A hand grabs her upper arm. Kristina Maria jerks away and turns around. She knows she is no beautiful sight at the moment, forehead sweating and upper lip drawn back against her gums.

"What are you after, creeping around today?"

Marta Vuori's bony hand squeezes her arm. That opera performance comes into her mind again and she thinks, All we need is the fancy dress.

"Leave the girl alone! What do you want with her?"

"Nothing. What's it got to do with you?"

They're speaking quietly in Finnish. Marta is the stronger, of course, and she pulls Kristina Maria with her up from the brewhouse toward the Vuoris' cottage. She's been the submissive one for a long time, Jerf's nice sister. But today it doesn't suit her to be pushed around and dragged by the arm. One look in the mirror above the kitchen dresser makes her burn with rage. That's what she looks like now. It's a long time since her mouth wasn't clamped shut. When she was a little girl, she sometimes laughed like Aili and Anna. There's been talk of getting her a new set of teeth, but without even looking at her, Edvin had said, "She'll get married all the same."

Wonder if Father would have stayed up in the tent, all but paralyzed with grief, if it had been ugly Ristin who was lost on the mountain?

"Well, what are you staring at? Get away from the mirror."

There's unease in Marta's voice; she senses the slow-burning hatred found only in the very patient.

"Listen," says Marta, arranging coffee cups. "We should help each other."

Her movements in the kitchen are awkward and impractical. The intimacy in her voice has been newly applied that day and is not particularly convincing.

"Get that policeman away from Rakisjokk," says Marta. "Do you think Per-Anti's reindeer would have been shot if he hadn't been here? What do you think will happen next?"

Kristina Maria doesn't reply. She is glancing out of the window along the shore, wondering about Anna.

"Just look at yourself," Marta goes on. "What are you going to do? people wonder. Until that policeman came, things were quite peaceful here. Get rid of him, I say."

"It started before then," says Kristina Maria.

"Aye, that business with Matti. Well, that's a long time ago now."

"No, I mean this summer."

She sounds stubborn and doesn't touch the coffee Marta has poured out.

"The day before the policeman came, Anna was packing her things because she was going to drive down south in her new car. She was planning to leave at the end of the week. I helped her air her clothes. Then I went home to cook a meal for Per-Anti. He was supposed to take the boat out for Henrik. When he got down to the jetty—I helped Per-Anti carry—along came Anna, white in the face and with hardly any luggage at all. She wanted to go on the boat and she said nothing to us. That's when it started."

"Drink your coffee. You're obsessed with her."

"It's true. Per-Anti says she got off the boat in Orjas without even saying hello to Anna Salminen, got into her new car, and drove off like a whirlwind. Then she came back the next day with those police people and not a word about going away has she said since."

"So she's the one who brought the police here, is she?" says Marta slowly.

"She doesn't like them."

"Oh, she's just pretending."

Marta thoughtfully stirs her coffee. A sticky flypaper is hanging in a spiral above the kitchen table, the orange strip dotted with dead flies and some that are still moving slightly. It occurs to Marta that it is difficult to leave Rakisjokk. She thinks about the headmaster who talks about leaving every year, about Anna who packed her cases, and about Erik Sjögren. Henrik always says, "Just you wait until I've got together enough money from the boat, two more summers. Then I'll buy a farm by the river Torne." He can talk. Ah, the smell of new-mown hay on the border islands in the river! Nothing ever comes of it. No, might as well accept it. It's only talk.

"I'm off now."

There's no point in trying to stop Kristina Maria. Her eyes keep flickering toward the window. Besides, Marta has heard the *Hork* down at the quay and she hurries over to the stove to fling a knob of lard into the frying pan for his pancake.

"Leave Anna alone."

Kristina Maria is already outside and probably doesn't hear her. Henrik comes in after a while, smelling of engine oil and sweat. One look from Marta is enough to send him over to the washbasin, whistling as he goes. It takes Marta's angular majesty to subdue a ladies' man like Henrik, though people couldn't believe it at first, attributing Henrik's infatuation to Marta's inheritance from her father.

"I've had Kristina Maria here."

"Aye, I can tell from the smell of coffee."

He tries sliding his hand over her hip and thigh, but she slaps the back of his hand with the spatula. Henrik puts his stinging hand to his mouth and looks up at her, eyes glazed with desire and gratitude.

"You should look to her a little," she says.

"Oh, I'd rather look—"

"Stop it. *Iʃtukaa* [Sit]."

"I'm already sitting down. What's up with Kristina Maria? Except that she's so ugly my mouth dries up looking at her."

"She's acting crazy today. Following Anna around and creeping up on her."

"Let them creep."

"I still think you should look to her."

"I heard."

Sullenly he eats his pancake. Just once he reaches out for Marta's waist as she goes past with the dish, but she wriggles away. Her eyes fall on the flypaper in the ceiling with an unfortunate fly twisting in the sticky mess.

"What are you staring at?"

"I . . ."

"What is it?"

"Henrik, when are you going to buy that farm in the Torne Valley?"

Momentarily, he sees how ugly she really is with her long, yellow face and colorless hair parted in the middle. Then the painful thought passes.

"Pikku tyttö parka [Poor little girl]," he says tenderly. "I'll buy it soon."

In the mosquito chorus of the evening, Kristina Maria sees David and Torsson setting off toward Kaittas, accompanied by Per-Anders, who is walking hunched up under a rucksack. He hasn't said a word about why they're going there. Well, she's not going to ask. Anna must also have seen them set off. Barely five minutes after they've disappeared into the forest, she can be seen by the corner of the headmaster's house, and she slips in among the birches so quickly that it requires sharp eyes to spot her. But Kristina Maria is prepared. She's already out of the door with her raincoat over her shoulders. Not for a moment is she going to look down toward the Vuoris'.

It is easy to see Anna and yet keep at a distance. Anna is wearing her yellow blouse, which can continually be glimpsed through the trees. Besides, her progress is awkward; she keeps stepping on dry twigs and pine cones. Kristina Maria doesn't have to make any effort to walk carefully. Soft, springy steps come naturally to her. For a moment she thinks Anna is following the three men up toward Kaittas. But as far as she knows, Anna has never been up there and wouldn't be able to find her way there alone.

Anna has a rucksack on her back. That is not what she

was carrying last night, Kristina Maria is sure. It is so big that she would have seen it. On the other hand, she thinks that what Anna carried last night is inside the rucksack. Anna is irresolute. After half a kilometer, she starts making her way out of the forest, following the slope upward. She seems not to know what she's looking for. Once she turns around, startled by a bird taking off, and Kristina Maria has to drop cautiously to her knees in the moss so as not to be seen.

The wind brings with it a damp, sour smell and Kristina Maria knows that they'll soon be out on the marsh. Anna doesn't know that. She stops, her back stiff and her head thrust forward, when the first tussock sways under her feet. But she doesn't try to turn back. After hesitating for a moment, she starts balancing on the tussocks, putting her feet down so gingerly that Kristina Maria has to laugh in her hiding place behind a pine tree. What is someone like her doing out on the marsh?

Anna's movements become more purposeful. She's looking for something, jumping back and forth. It would be dangerous to go any nearer now. She might change direction at any moment. Not until it's almost too late does Kristina Maria see what Anna is up to.

She is squatting down with the rucksack in front of her, rummaging in it. All around her, the water glimmers black in the holes. Oh, she's going to dump it! Kristina Maria cries out and starts leaping toward her. Her screech is jarring and perhaps frightens Anna more than need be.

Anna thinks it is some animal crying out. She flings her arms around the rucksack, trying not to lose her balance. Not until Kristina Maria's sweaty white face is right above her does she realize who it is.

"What have you got there? A bark bag—"

Anna has never suspected how strong those small brown fingers can be. They both tug at the rucksack, breathing heavily.

"Don't act daft," Anna gasps. "Are you out of your mind?"

But Kristina Maria jabs her elbow straight into Anna's midriff so that she staggers and her feet slide into the water. As her boots fill with cold marsh water and the smell of decay rises to her nostrils, she is seized with panic. She takes a few tentative steps, but the sucking water is soon above her knees.

"Don't move or you'll sink even deeper."

Kristina Maria states this calmly and does not hold out a hand to help her.

"Help me, Kristina Maria! For God's sake!"

The entire marsh now seems to Kristina Maria to be swaying and a powerful voice is bellowing agitatedly in the distance. She turns around and sees Henrik Vuori leaping agilely from tussock to tussock toward her. She quickly holds out a hand to Anna and laughs with embarrassment. But Henrik is already there, pushing her aside.

"*Suksi helvettiin siitä* [Get the hell out of here]! Come on, Anna. What are you up to, you girls?"

"My rucksack!" says Anna.

Kristina Maria has retreated from them, at first slowly balancing between the glimmering water holes, then faster and faster, glancing over her shoulder. By the time Vuori has got Anna up beside him, Kristina Maria has already disappeared.

"There, *pikku tyttö* [little girl]. You're soaking wet. You're shaking. What's all this about? What did Kristina Maria want from you?"

"I don't know," says Anna, her teeth chattering.

"Come on then. Would you like me to carry you? Oh, sure I can—you're as light and soft as a kitten."

He hauls Anna and her rucksack off with him and finally tips her down on dry land. Evil-smelling water is running out of her boots and her skirt is sticking to her body in a way that makes Henrik's hand tremble as he gets out a cigarette and lights it for her. Anna ties up the rucksack and empties the water out of her boots.

"Now, just tell me what you two were up to."

"Kristina Maria's gone weird. It was nothing. She's been staring at me all day and then I thought I'd go for a walk . . ."

"On the marsh?"

"You know I've got no sense of direction. She must have followed me and then, I don't know, somehow she pushed me."

Henrik is sitting with his head on one side, listening with a smile. His pale blue eyes are friendly.

"Somehow she pushed you? You know, that doesn't sound too good."

"No." Anna runs her hand down her wet skirt. "Henrik," she says seriously, "I might have been there for good."

"Oh, it wasn't that bad. But the way you kept floundering about!"

"You see . . . she saw me last night."

"Last night?"

"Yes, I couldn't sleep. I walked past their house last night. After what happened to those reindeer, she doesn't know what to think."

Anna has hitherto felt that Henrik is on her side, but now a slight chill comes into his voice.

"But you can't shoot, can you?"

"No, not at all," Anna says, stammering. "I hardly know how to fire a gun."

Henrik pushes his cigarette end into the moss and grinds it around, busy for a long time putting it out.

"Well, that reindeer business isn't as bad as all that. But that the bastard should only injure . . . didn't know any better," he mumbles.

"Henrik, are you going to tell the police? About last night?"

Anna's voice is softer than he has ever heard it. She runs her hand down his arm, but the hand is cold and wet and he shrinks away.

"Aye." He gets up roughly. "Now let's take your rucksack and go. Lucky I went after Kristina Maria. Marta told me I ought to look to her."

Henrik speaks not a word on the way home through the forest. The evening is chilly and there's a smell of snow on the wind from the mountain. The plumes of smoke from the village chimneys are restless.

"Bloody awful weather on the way, I reckon," Henrik mumbles to himself as they go past the headmaster's house.

Eklind is on his knees in his little stonecrop bed.

"Look at him, growing flowers with his backside to the mountain wind. He must be crazy not to leave this place."

Erik Sjögren is at his weather station when Henrik goes back home. He's reading off the 7 P.M. temperature and his papers are turning themselves over in the wind.

"Any day now they'll mention us on the radio," he says.

"They do that every day on those weather frauds."

"Aye, but specially. It's going to be cold. Perhaps the

coldest place in the country. We haven't had that since last winter."

"Yes, we have."

"No," says Erik vehemently. "Don't you think I know my business?" He waves his papers about, spitting with fervor.

"You poor loon," says Vuori. "We were the coldest place in the country last March. That was the night Matti died. The strangest weather ever. First it snowed for hours, then the cold set in and the temperature dropped so many degrees, I thought there was something wrong with the thermometers. But you wouldn't know about that."

Erik lowers his papers. He's frightened and confused. Vuori is usually reliable and speaks his mind. Try as he may, Sjögren can't remember anything special about the temperature that night.

"Because you forgot to take a reading," says Henrik with a smile. "I had to do it for you."

8. THE PASSESADJE

"Switch off your transmitters! Screen off the area! Green light for the squad leaders!"

David made a second round of Jerf's house to assure himself that there was no one anywhere near. A tousled cat at first flatly refused to clear the area, but finally went away with one hind leg irritably kicking in the air.

"Be quiet for a moment now."

Torsson was mulling over a few thoughts, his hands sweaty, a bundle of papers spread out in front of him. After much musing, he occasionally scribbled something down.

"I think I've checked for bugs now," David said to him. "Though I have a feeling there are ears flapping in every bush here. Are you ready? How does it feel?"

"Try to keep your mouth shut for a while."

It was early in the afternoon, long before the headmaster's coffee party. The only life left in the cottage after David's raid was buzzing around the lampshade. Torsson reached out, but at that moment Jerf's eight-day clock thundered out the quarter hour with such authority that he jerked his hand back and sucked it.

"Are you a coward?" asked David accusingly.

"Am I?" said Torsson timidly.

"Now then, come on! No beating about the bush. Remember, this is your duty."

The effect of that word on Torsson was that his eyes disappeared and he bared his teeth. For the second time, he reached out and turned the handle, then lifted the receiver.

"Orjas!" a voice yelled out of fluffy knitting wool.

"This is 36B. Can you put me through to town? To the police station."

"Is that Per-Anti?" the wool asked.

"No, it's—get me the town! The police station!" Torsson bellowed.

"Heavens!"

There was a click and a brief buzzing sound.

"Has something happened?"

"Is that the police station?"

"No, be with you in a moment. What—"

"If you listen in, we'll cut your ears off," David bawled helpfully into the mouthpiece. Torsson pushed him away.

The hollow sound ceased and soon after came a voice saying, "Police station." Torsson asked to speak to the chief of police and, while the clicks went on, he wiped his sweaty left hand against his trouser leg. David had expected a roar as if from a lion's den. He was surprised when a wearily creaking voice at the other end admitted that he was the chief of police and he wasn't enjoying it.

"Torsson here," said Torsson. "I'm in Rakisjokk. No, not Eskilstuna this time. No . . . bad idea, no doubt." He sent a look up into outer space and went on, "I'm phoning because they've shot a couple of reindeer up here."

He started an elaborate explanation of the events of the night and got his syntax into such a tangle that David had to come to his assistance in an undertone.

". . . his *own* rifle. And the scarf, don't forget the scarf."

"No, it's nobody. Just someone who—"

David listened open-mouthed. He managed to catch a few creaking words.

"Yes, shoot reindeer, that's one thing they *can* do."

He did not find out what they couldn't do.

"And they're telling lies, too," said Torsson. "Lies, aye."

The chief of police let it be known that he didn't think that would merit a front-page headline.

"They've been lying about when Matti Olsson died. He died on the Saturday before I came up here in March. Matti, aye—the one who died. And not in the place they first told me, either. Whose benefit? I don't know." He wiped his forehead. "I suppose they can't help themselves. And I don't believe he got there unaided."

Torsson made the last remark as if it was his duty to

report this, but not his place to make sure it had been understood.

"Has he fallen asleep?" David asked uneasily.

"No, he's just having a wee rest. He gets so tired of Norrbotten sometimes, he says."

"Find out who it was that shot them."

"Aye."

"And you're not on holiday any longer."

"No."

After this there was a click, a piece of music of the spheres, and then the voice from Orjas: "Have you finished now?"

"No. Get me the police station again."

Torsson asked to speak to Fredriksson. Every man is the master of some poor wretch, David thought as Torsson authoritatively asked him to find the records of the interrogations in March dealing with what Rakisjokk had been up to after the party.

While Fredriksson was off the phone, David asked, "What do you want them for? Surely you don't think you can get anything out of all those half-lies?"

"Well," said Torsson, getting paper and pencil ready, "if I'm to find out who shot those reindeer, then—"

"Then you'll have to make a detour via Matti and that girl Aili?"

"Aye, something like that."

"You'll never catch her, all the same."

"So you think she killed Matti?"

"Not at all. But I know she got rid of the Aili girl, and I think Matti found out and went and lay down in the snow. That's the kind of thing that would make Matti give up. But we'll never nail her. She's as cold as ice and nothing touches her. I thought I'd stay in her vicinity and torment her with the reminder that I knew. But it's not working. I'm the one who'll fall to pieces in the end."

"You poor little thing," said Torsson mildly, and then, "Hello, yes? Have you got them there? Start with the schoolmaster."

Torsson had written headings down on his paper and under the first one, HEADMASTER, he now put in: "Played mah-jongg until half past ten. Went to his house, sat down to read a book. Went to bed, hour unknown, but late."

"Pah!" said David.

"ANNA RYD," Torsson wrote. "Mah-jongg. To bed just after half past ten on the upper floor of the schoolmaster's house. P-A JERF, drinking until half past eleven, went home. Slept alone. KRIST. MAR.," he wrote, "slept at the school with the children. MARTA VUORI, home just after half past ten. Slept. SJÖGREN, with Matti in the school-house until half past eleven. Returned sometime after one, maybe nearer two o'clock. Went home and fell asleep."

"Pah, pah, pah—if you want my opinion," said David.

"You can put them back now. No, don't even think about it. You couldn't handle it."

He finished off the conversation with a pitying shake of the head and gathered up his papers.

"I suppose you think this is all highly interesting?" said David.

"Nah."

"Don't forget they lied about when he died and where. There's nothing to stop them lying all along the line."

"The question is why they all lied."

"Not at all. It's totally banal. They simply can't help it. Remember what Matti wrote to me: 'Up here, falsehood walks around on two legs.' Well, myth, if you like. But I sensed he meant lies. Common or garden lies." David struck the bowl of his pipe on the table so that the flies scurried up and completed the pattern of dots on the lampshade.

"Have you finished with the phone?"

Jerf was standing behind them. What he hated about this place, David thought, was the way people kept materializing out of nowhere. You could never be sure how long they'd been there. Per-Anders had come from the shed, and for what must be the tenth time that day, he washed his hands in the basin.

"Per-Anti, I've been assigned to investigate the shooting," said Torsson.

"Who by?" he asked sullenly.

"My boss."

"Well, he's not the boss of my reindeer and I haven't made a complaint."

"Don't you want to find out who did it?"

Jerf's eyes narrowed. He didn't answer.

"And then there's this Matti business."

"What about Matti?"

"And Aili."

Per-Anders padded across and looked at him. "Aili? I don't understand."

Torsson told him about the birch-bark bag they'd seen in Anna's possession. He told him what was inside it. He spoke as calmly as if he had been describing a briefcase with lost property, and he never once looked at Per-Anders.

Per-Anders slowly turned toward the wall, supporting himself against it with one hand. His slim back was shaking.

"Go easy, Torsson," David mumbled. "Imagine if it was your sister."

"Don't . . . don't tell Father," Per-Anders stammered without looking up. "You mustn't go and tell Father. He loved Aili . . . a lot." He swung around to reveal a tear-stained face, then suddenly clenched his fists. "Anna—that bitch! I'll—"

"Oh, no, you won't," said Torsson.

"I'll be happy to help you," said David. "Just tell me what we have to do."

"Quiet!" Torsson snapped. "And leave Anna alone. As for your father, he is just the person we're going to talk to."

"You wouldn't!" Per-Anders hissed. "Do you want to kill him?"

David looked thoughtfully at him. Wasn't there an element of cool self-control in his abandonment to despair? Or had his feelings been blunted by everything that had happened since last night's shooting?

"I think your father knows more about this than anyone else," said Torsson. "No doubt he has his reasons for staying up there in the tent. And don't forget it was from his place Matti came that Saturday evening in March."

"And you think he'll say anything?" said Per-Anders. "Father's not like me. We can't even count on seeing him. He hasn't had much time for Swedes this last year."

Per-Anders spat out the last words as if he, too, were getting tired of Swedish people. He started striding uneasily up and down the room, his fingers nervously playing with the buttons on his red checked shirt.

"Oh, well then. I suppose we'd better go up there. This evening. If things are as you say. But if he doesn't know about it, I don't know what I'm going to do with you!

You'll get thrown out of Rakisjokk, you'll see." His whining voice held little threat. "I've no more time for you now. Go away! First I've got to sort out all that business from last night—oh, Christ, I'm sick of these flies! Go on, get out!"

As they stumbled down Jerf's steps, it was David who felt ashamed. Torsson's expression was calm and devoid of intelligence.

It was six o'clock when they emerged from the forest by the Kaittas tents. The scene was as lifeless as when they had last seen it, and the cold now creeping up the valley had hung light white shrouds of mist between the birches.

Per-Anders hallooed, "Father!"

He called out in Sami, shouting his father's first name. It sounded like Etvina. His voice dropped at the end into a low, doglike howl, then settled in the mist.

"He's in," said Per-Anders suddenly and started walking toward the big main tent. How he knew his father was in, David couldn't make out. The dog, still with the piece of rope swinging from its neck, showed itself behind a rock and barked at them. It came closer as they walked up to the tent and snapped at David's leg with its front teeth. David was stiff with fear and cold and walked with his legs close together. Per-Anders kicked at the dog and it ran squealing into the forest.

"We won't see any more of it now. Father's always had nasty, sneaky dogs." His voice was low. "Stay here," he said, and made to enter the tent. "I'm not sure he'll want to see you."

They tried to distinguish the voices inside, but it

sounded as if Per-Anders was doing all the talking. Shivering, they noticed the smoke thickening and the smell of coffee beginning to waft out in their direction.

"Does one have to request an audience with this reindeer pope?" David grumbled. "What's so special about the old man?"

"Ssh," said Torsson warningly. "He's sure to have ears."

"May they fall off so his cap slides down over his neb. I'm cold."

They were kept waiting a long time before Per-Anders stuck out a solemn face and beckoned them in. David entered first. The tent was large, with dark corners. At first he could see nothing but the fire burning brightly on the hearth and the coffee kettle bouncing on its hook. You might think the old man had been expecting guests. Large armfuls of fresh birch covered the floor, reindeer skins swaying softly on top. The smell of the leaves was sharp and fresh. David greeted the darkest corner and tucked his legs under him.

When Per-Anders threw a large birch log on the fire and poked it with a stick so that it flared up, David could make out the old man in the corner, the smallest, most desiccated old man he had ever seen. He was dressed in the old-fashioned way in a tunic of faded wool with a great many ribbon trimmings. How he could have fathered the twice as tall Per-Anders in his flannel shirt and jeans was a mystery. His skin had darkened and shriveled over his skull, which gave his face sharp, chiseled features. That was all David could register before his eyes started watering and smarting from the smoke and he had to rub them with his knuckles.

"You'll get used to it," Per-Anders comforted him, seeing his predicament. "Keep down. The air's best there."

Torsson came crawling across the reindeer skins and, puffing and blowing, made his way over to Edvin Jerf. He politely shook hands and greeted him and David was ashamed for a moment. It was obvious that Per-Anders had not yet said anything about why they had come. Edvin was not put out. He was busy looking at them and he seldom blinked. Small and shriveled, he looked like a bird that had flown up into the corner and perched there. Per-Anders clearly held him in great respect and addressed him in mumbling Sami. It appeared that he had been given permission to serve them coffee.

David was handed a flawless porcelain cup with a rosebud pattern on it. He was feeling increasingly confused. From his rucksack Per-Anders took the things he had brought for his father—a bag of coffee and packets of tobacco. There was also a loaf of raisin bread that Kristina Maria had baked before her great rage had overcome her. Per-Anders started slicing it.

"I think David's been silenced," said Torsson teasingly, and Per-Anders translated into Sami, presumably out of politeness, for it was quite unnecessary. The old man gave a sudden laugh and the dry sound filled the tent. He understood perfectly well—it was evident from his clear gaze moving from one to the other. But he had no desire to speak Swedish today, or Finnish. He shook his head and smiled at Torsson.

"Buggered if I could live in a fish smokery like this for a single day!" David exclaimed, having considered ten ways of acting against his nature and finally giving up.

"Father says it's good for one's health." Per-Anders

hastened to translate the almost inaudible mumble from the old man. "The body becomes tough and doesn't smell."

David blinked in the smoky air, wondering whether he had heard right. Wasn't that a sighing titter from the corner?

The coffee was scalding hot and proffered with both sugar (boiled gray) and salt. David did not mistake them, but Torsson did, and then endured the taste and Per-Anders's searching looks without a word. They began to realize that it was going to take a long time before the reason for their visit was brought up. The sky was already changing color in the smoke vent at the top—the indigo turning green and the cold making the smoke descend in despair. Per-Anders talked courteously about Rakisjokk, the many tourists and the *Hork*, which was having engine trouble. Then in a roundabout way he began to approach the events of the night before. He recounted the fate of the two reindeer. The old man uttered not a single sound. He must have heard the shots, and might have got there before his son did. At least, he didn't have as far to go. Now they could hear Per-Anders getting closer to the matter in hand. He went on entirely in Sami, putting down the stick he'd been fiddling with and automatically turning the spout of the coffee kettle so that it pointed toward the back recess. A spout facing the tent entrance—up here in Kaittas, he didn't like it, though down in Rakisjokk he quite happily walked under ladders and killed spiders.

Torsson and David leaned back, listening to the drowsy mumble, but when the name Aili was first mentioned, they both looked up. At that moment the fire flared up. A glowing spark shot out toward Edvin Jerf, landing on the back of his hand. How badly he was burned was not clear. He was sitting painfully still with downcast eyes while the ember blackened on his hand. David cried out and wriggled forward to brush the crumb of charcoal off that dry, bony hand. Being so close to the old man that he could smell the smoke from his clothes, he felt embarrassed. Yet Edvin Jerf never moved.

Cautiously, Per-Anders went on. He mentioned Aili's name repeatedly and tears began running down his cheeks. He pointed at Torsson and David, then at himself, and explained. Finally he fell silent, out of breath, and wiped his cheeks with the bandanna he had around his neck, while waiting for his father to answer.

They had to wait. The old man was struggling with something there in the dark. His breathing was uneven and his hands fiddled with the cup and pipe. Hope the old boy doesn't have a stroke, David thought anxiously. He was becoming attached to this little collection of smoked bones that was Per-Anders's father. Slowly it grew darker inside the tent. A damp birch log hissed in the fire and Per-Anders reached out for another, drier log.

"*Ei* [No]!"

That came from Edvin. Per-Anders dropped the log as obediently and quickly as if he'd been a dog. The old man wanted darkness.

"*Ei mitään* [Nothing] . . ."

He got no further. Per-Anders crawled over to him and they started speaking in Sami. The other two could hear that Per-Anders was telling the old man something. They caught the names Aili and, at long last, Matti. They couldn't see the old man, only Per-Anders's flushed face and animated eyes reflecting the glow from the fire. Per-Anders asked only one question and the old man seemed to find it difficult to answer. He stammered and they saw his hands fumbling over Per-Anders's back. Suddenly Per-Anders turned around and crawled over to David.

"You'd better go," he whispered. "Father's unhappy. You'd better go."

He crawled back to the corner and the monotonous mumbling went on.

It was a shock coming out into the fresh air. David's eyes were red-rimmed and watering badly. The cold had taken hold and the sun looked inflamed and distant.

"Don't you ever wear anything other than that thin jacket?" Torsson inquired.

"Yes, I wear a corduroy one in winter."

"Do you have to? Is it meant to look bohemian and artistic?"

But his voice was dull and there was no reason to continue their bickering. They retreated to the edge of the forest and sat down in the grass.

"They always start talking in Sami when things are getting warm."

"Aye. No doubt they have their reasons."

"Did you understand any of it?"

"Nah."

"But he looked upset. Wonder what hurt most?"

"The *passesadje*," said Torsson.

"Eh?"

"The *passesadje*. That's all I could make out. Toward the end he stammered the word several times."

"What's that?"

A glint entered Torsson's eyes, but it wasn't the usual one. It was a black glint of fear.

"Place of sacrifice."

David stared at him. "Say that again," he said. "Am I dreaming?"

"No," said Torsson emphatically. "That's what he said."

He groped in his pocket for his cigarettes, at the same time glancing over his shoulder toward the tent. The smoke trickling out of the hole was very thin. Torsson licked his lips.

"It's the kind of place they had in the olden days," he said. "Usually in a valley, or some place you can only get to through a narrow pass. They're dangerous places. All manner of . . . you know . . . evil there."

"Torsson," said David seriously, "have you gone off your head?"

"Don't get me wrong. I mean, that's what the old people believed. In the olden days, that is. So they had their places of sacrifice at the entrance to that kind of valley. They were so sacred that only the shamans were allowed in. Nowadays I don't suppose anyone makes sacrifices or even believes in the old gods."

"I should hope not. Try to sound a bit more rational, if you don't mind." Torsson's mumbling voice and lowered eyes were getting on David's nerves.

"But veneration for those old places still lingers. And the fear of them," Torsson went on.

"Do you really mean that? Seriously? Among people who have refrigerators and radios in their winter quarters and take internal flights instead of moving with the herd?"

"Aye," was all Torsson said. After a while he went on, almost agitatedly, "I do mean it. Do you go barging into church with your hat on?"

"No," said David, "that's true. But that's not because

I'm afraid. The worst that could happen would be that a considerate verger might point out the error of my ways."

"Fear of those places is probably not so stupid. They're often in hollows in valleys, where really stinking weather can form in next to no time. You can't expect to escape lightly if you're caught in a storm there."

David plucked impatiently at the grass. It seemed to him that Torsson was talking from behind a thick glass wall.

"So the superstition is logical—up to a point?" said David. "Gods and evil spirits are a euphemism for bad weather."

"Or it's the bad weather that's a euphemism for something." Torsson shook his head like a gloomy dog. "It wasn't superstition, for that matter," he added, "it was religion."

David said nothing, feeling that he had walked into church with his hat on after all.

"Now, don't go all gloomy," he said, nudging Torsson lightly. "Think about Eskilstuna for a while and it'll pass. What did the old man say about the *passesadje,* or what the hell it's called?"

"I don't know. I've learned only a few words of Sami. All I know is that there's supposed to be a place like that up there somewhere."

He nodded toward the mountain without looking up. David stared, his gaze climbing up above the sickly mauve color of the birches and getting lost in a belt of reddish brown higher up.

"Suppose, Torsson," he mumbled, "that this is Mount Tabor?"

"Eh?"

"The site of the Transfiguration," said David, but got

hurriedly to his feet when he heard Per-Anders Jerf's quiet footsteps behind him.

Per-Anders's face was quite expressionless. "You'd better go home. Father doesn't want to see you anymore."

"I understand it made him unhappy," mumbled David. "I'm sorry . . ."

"Well, you'd better go home." Jerf's voice was childishly stubborn.

"But what did he have to say?"

"Nothing."

His tone of voice was so dismissive that David shut his mouth.

"It'd be best if you left Rakisjokk altogether," Jerf said, his thin lips tightening. "As far as Matti's concerned, you'd best let him lie where he is. If you call yourself a friend of his."

The scorn in his voice reminded David of something, of Anna Ryd's hard eyes and the little hand that had clutched his sleeve.

"I'm saying this in all seriousness," said Per-Anders. "Up to now I haven't lied or deceived you quite as much as the others have. So you'd do well to listen to me."

He turned and started walking back toward the tent, clearly intending to stay up there.

"But what about Matti?"

"You didn't know him," said Per-Anders calmly.

The smell of smoke from his clothes remained hanging in the air after he had gone.

David shivered in the cold and set off walking, Torsson behind him. The dog slunk ahead of them for a while and, when they had gone into the forest, it hurled a few barks after them.

9. A MESSAGE FROM THE GODS

The name was a mouthful of unpronounceable sounds, eight syllables long.

"Kuottatjåkk . . . kott . . ." David attempted, as Torsson's grubby forefinger ran along the row of letters.

"Never mind," said Torsson. "That's where it is, anyhow. What do you think?"

David had no thoughts at all at that time of the morning. The gray daylight and the cold induced in him a sense of infinity—he could imagine a Hades full of vacant souls fluttering past each other in an endless morning shiver.

"Don't fall asleep," said Torsson firmly.

"Well, it's not far," David mumbled. "We ought to be able to find it."

"You don't know what you're talking about. But that doesn't matter."

Torsson folded up the map. An unnoticed mosquito was squashed flat against the South Peak, appearing to be the size of an elephant by the scale of the map.

"We simply can't take anyone with us. Depends on what we find."

He was looking dreamy, as if imagining buried treasure at the place of sacrifice. David shivered and started lacing up his boots. By questionable means, they had acquired supplies of food and drink and packed them into their rucksacks. Their intention was to leave early, before any smoke would be emerging from the village chimneys. Torsson was worried—he knew they oughtn't to go without a guide. However, David appeared comfortingly unruffled. In fact, he was so sleepy that he was barely conscious, unable even to remark on the unreasonable number of eyelets in one pair of boots.

Torsson locked the door and they set off. Cold chimneys were outlined against the lake and the sky. No dog barked. Torsson went on ahead and worked himself up into a sweat. David stumbled along after him, his gaze fixed on the ground. Their silence was that of a thirty-year marriage. At the first spur of the marsh, Torsson spoke.

"How are you feeling?"

A few kilometers into the forest, David replied, "What?"

Torsson stopped to look at the map. He regarded the compass, coldly trembling in its little house.

"We'll have to go around Kaittas. It's a detour, but that can't be helped. The old man mustn't see us."

They came out so close to Kaittas that they could see the camp down in the valley with its two thin columns of smoke. The dog with the silly curl in its tail was scampering around in the cotton grass, but it didn't hear them. They were now in the mauve belt of birches David had seen from below Kaittas. Inchworms had attacked the trees and turned them this shriveled heart-disease color. Although the waterlogged osier swamp lay ahead of them, they were glad to get out of that mortuary atmosphere.

The squelching of his boots in the black swamp woke David. "Crikey!" he said. "Is this wise?"

"No," Torsson replied, his breathing becoming increasingly asthmatic. There were damp half-moons now under his shirtsleeves and irritating trickles of sweat down his forehead.

"Just think," said David, "maybe she took this route."

"Who?"

"Aili."

Torsson gave him a swift glance over the shoulder and plodded on. David couldn't tell whether he was listening or not.

"They were having a party in the village. Kristina Maria may have been frying grouse in butter, and I'm sure Matti must have been putting up decorations—ornamental archways and that kind of thing. He was good at that. And then she just walked off. Dirtied her fine skirt in the swamp and got her feet wet and cold. She probably went through that dead birch forest we saw just now. I can almost hear the silver tinkling in the silence. Do you think she was meeting someone?"

"I don't know."

"Do you think we'll find out?"

"Aye."

"Up here? In Kuotta . . . tjo . . . kuo . . ."

"Maybe."

They had reached a windswept plateau and David fell silent. The large heads of the globe flowers were swaying in the wind. Far down below he could see the lakes glimmering like cold mirrors, the Rakisjaure an icily sharp knife wound darkened by passing shadows of cloud. The wind had torn the sky apart, but the occasional blue patches looked cold. They crouched down in the heather and took their first coffee break. David looked sadly at Torsson as he settled his considerable weight on the pink flowers.

Torsson took out the map and started studying it. On all fours in the scrub, he peered this way and that, mumbling gloomy guesses at the positions of the mountain. peaks. They agreed they were just where the squashed mosquito had left one of its legs on the paper. With some energy, they tried to convince each other they really did know their position, until David tactlessly exclaimed:

"What if we never find our way?"

He suddenly felt very cold and diminutive in the wind, which came whistling down from the mountain like a harsh breath from the ice age blowing a sardonic laugh against his back.

"Huh," said Torsson, looking timidly around.

The brown and blue mountain wall streaked with white glacier teeth now seemed so close to them that its shadow might have been the cause of the chill in their backsides. But once they left their resting place, their feet started taking them downhill and another valley opened up. Yellow with mud, a glacial river raced along it, the sound soon turning into a ringing note in their ears. Directly below their feet, the river kept disgorging chunks of ice into the blue mirror of a lake, the floes swirling and tumbling around in the water.

"Look over to the right instead," said Torsson. His voice sounded bewildered, almost solemn. "There it is."

Long and narrow, it extended between the flanks of the mountains. All thickness in the air had retreated and settled darkly blue at the end of the valley. At a distance, the entrance to the pass looked to them like the eye of a needle. They started walking through the cotton grass, placing their feet with caution on the marshy ground. Then they came to drier ground, easier to walk on, with reindeer trails running parallel. For every hundred meters they covered, the valley appeared to move a little farther off. It kept gliding away under its dark blue cap, the shadows of clouds moving uneasily across the level ground.

"What if we ran into someone?" David sighed. "Wouldn't that be nice?"

"You're joking. I wouldn't want to meet anyone with a reason for coming here."

Suddenly the valley was no longer a mirage. The narrow pass lay in front of them, blocked by a large rock tipped on its side. The silence was like padding.

"Well then . . . we'll go on in, shall we?" said Torsson, not moving.

"You first," David said with eager politeness.

Torsson laughed, the sound dry with no echo. He had begun to feel cold and pulled on his windbreaker over his sweat-soaked shirt. It took him several minutes to carry out the operation, then hoist his rucksack back on again. David stood still, his eyes on the ground, waiting.

"Yoohoo!" Torsson cried. "Take a deep breath and off we go."

Noisily but quite unnecessarily, he blew his nose—a kind of exorcism, David presumed—then eased his way in past the edge of the rock. David followed him like a shadow, sensing that they ought not to lose contact.

"This looks just like where we've come from."

It did. But there were no reindeer trails. The tufts of cotton grass were immobile in the stillness. The valley looked long when seen from the opening, then disappeared through the magic of perspective into the dark mountainsides. The stone blocking the entrance had an overhang and in the shadow below it lay a collection of stones placed in a semicircle.

"So this is your actual . . . the actual *passesadje,*" said Torsson in an unnecessarily loud voice as he pointed at the stones. He made a sweeping gesture with his arm and looked around like a tour guide at the dead landscape.

"Those bones . . ." David muttered vaguely.

"Of course," cried Torsson. "Reindeer bones. Sacrificed. Sure to be ancient. They're quite white. Look, they've had the sense to split them and suck out the marrow first. The gods can always put new flesh on bones and fill them with marrow."

He added the last remark in an almost ingratiating tone which made David look around.

"Ridiculous!" David said suddenly. "The whole thing is ridiculous."

"Yes, isn't it?" Torsson agreed, and they both fell silent.

David lit his pipe. They moved away from the *passesadje*

to take a look around them. Toward the valley was a large area of untrampled ground, here and there a ragged cairn of stones, impossible to say whether made by humans or not. Gradually their sense of insecurity faded. They adjusted to the stillness and stumped noisily around studying the ground. Exactly what they were looking for was not stated. Sweaty, they turned back to the rock and stood, feet apart, slightly out of breath, in front of the circle of stones. Their shape interested David. He wanted to hold them in his hand and feel their roundness.

"They're stone gods," said Torsson. "Idols. Ridiculous."

David reached out a hand.

"Don't!" Torsson tittered with embarrassment.

"What?"

"Leave them alone. They've got nothing to do with us."

But David had already seized the prettiest one. From its soft curves, he took it to be a small stone goddess. It felt cool and hard to the touch. At that moment two or three splashes of rain landed on the back of David's hand, and that was all the warning they were given.

The wind came racing around from the northwest with a howl of glee and hurled a shower of ice-blended curses straight into their astonished, upturned faces. They swung around and turned their backs to it. David dropped the stone.

"Hey, that was quick! Did you notice the weather about to turn?"

But Torsson didn't hear him. He was struggling with the rucksack past the rock and stumbling on with the wind behind him.

"We must get out of here!" he shouted. "Hurry, and keep close."

In rising wind and rain, they struggled on. David suddenly noticed his leg muscles tensing and bracing against the slippery rock surfaces.

"Wrong way, Torsson!" he shouted. "We're going uphill. It ought to be level."

"Oh, shut up," said Torsson, rudely confident. He struggled on in a wind that seemed to be coming from all directions at once. The rain was heavier now, the wind driving it mixed with snow along the ground. They had to turn back when a rock wall appeared, black and jagged in the murk ahead of them. In the other direction they caught a brief glimpse of a view—an ice-cold mosaic of black and gray lakes and immobile mountain ridges ripping the drifting clouds into shreds.

David was having regrets. Stiff and soaking wet, he was cursing with all the breath he could muster. Moreover, he was beset by the constant feeling that they were going upward, but Torsson wouldn't listen to his shouts. Maybe he couldn't hear them. David closed his eyes and stumbled on, then suddenly saw their journey in front of him as if in an aerial photograph—saw them stumbling around in ever crazier circles, two flyspecks in an infinitely beautiful landscape of stone and ice.

The spirits of the stone gods are capricious. Quite suddenly they turned their attention to some other frolic. Or else they rolled indolently over in the warmth of the tent of Sami paradise, Saiva, and forgot the intruders. The wind retreated into its lairs again and the clouds had emptied their contents. The entire storm ended in a clammy fog—though it was hard to tell clouds from fog up here—lazily drifting away over the peaks and dissolving.

"Where the hell are we?"

Torsson stood open-mouthed, water running off his

head as he glared around, balancing uneasily on the sharp stones. All around them there was nothing to be seen but stones, drifts and petrified waves of slippery stones.

"And such ugly stones at that," said David quietly.

With infinite caution, they started to make their way across the pitfalls of the moraine in that most ugly and sterile of landscapes.

Neither tried to persuade the other that he knew where they were. They were simply enormously grateful when they spotted the first green patch of moss. They reached the bottom of a valley two hours later, and it was frighteningly unfamiliar. Sun and warmth started returning. In the first tussock of heather, David flung himself down full length and stared up at the sky, now an enchanting seaside blue—but as false as a girl's eye. He knew that now. Beside him was a stalk of lousewort gently spreading a scent of roses.

Torsson had collected up an armful of osier scrub and set it alight. It didn't give off much heat but sent up thick white smoke which would be visible kilometers away, should anyone be interested in them. They ate and made an attempt to dry their clothes in the sun by spreading them out on the ground.

"Who'd have thought that they'd get so annoyed just because I touched that stupid little stone," said David. He felt lighthearted and in a mood to challenge a whole Olympus of gods to an argument. But at the same time he knew he would never again in his life put his hand on any wretched stone in a *passesadje*.

They wandered around on tender feet for most of the afternoon, seeing no other sign of life than a reindeer herd moving like a patterned shadow on a distant mountain slope. They gazed at a landscape that showed them only the fixed smile of a complete stranger.

"Huh," said Torsson. By this stage they were limiting their speech to the sounds from which the Pithecanthropus people had formed their grammar.

Sluggishly, David followed the direction of Torsson's forefinger. A narrow column of gray smoke was rising above the tops of the birches and winding restlessly up into the sky. Five minutes' limping walk revealed a valley, and on its slope the pointed cone of the Kaittas tent. Although they were close enough to see the wire netting over the turf roof, they decided against. Edvin and Per-Anders ought to live a while longer in happy ignorance of Torsson's ability to understand Sami.

They circled it the same way they had done on the way up, and eventually arrived back in Rakisjokk. Their appearance would have frightened small children, had there been any there, but as it was, Kristina Maria was the one to see them. She clapped her hands together and closed her wide-open mouth with a synchronized snap.

"Heavens above, look at you two! Have you been through a dishwasher?" she cried, for she was a modern young woman with a dream.

The fact that Kristina Maria dragged them with her into the school hall and put on the cocoa owed less to friendliness than to her desire to procure some entertainment for Rakisjokk assembled there for the evening. She displayed them with a treasure hunter's delight, and they were met by the introspective smiles of warm and dry people around the fire.

"You might've died up there," said Eklind, with a cool note of reproach.

"Unfortunately we were unable to arrange such scenes of joy for you," said David. "We're crazy about life, Torsson and I."

The company watched with interest his attempts to light a wad of soggy tobacco. Curiosity is no virtue in Rakisjokk, so it was with very courteous circumlocutions that they approached the subject of what exactly Torsson and David had been looking for on their mountain hike. But the two men let nothing escape them except dark swamp water from their shoes. David began to feel like a person of some significance.

"I've seen a thing or two in my life," he said, rolling his eyes, "but nothing like . . . The hair on my chest has grown five millimeters, but then I've been challenging the gods."

Torsson realized that all that was needed now was a female sigh of admiration for David to start making up ballads about their great deeds. Tenderly, he said, "The poor wretch whimpered like a puppy in a shower."

A quiet smile hummed through the school hall and David blew his nose.

"It seems a bit odd that you're about to leave here just when so many strange things keep happening," said Marta Vuori suddenly, glancing up at her husband. "Aren't you going to—"

"Leave the gentlemen alone now. I'll give you a *puoristkokse* to warm you up. See, Kristina Maria, I can speak Sami, Swede that I am."

Henrik Vuori unscrewed the cap of a small bottle and poured some of the contents into their cups of cocoa.

"Mm. Almost like that professor last summer. Per-Anti always gets worried when he thinks Englishmen are coming, but that professor was so nice. 'Great subtlety characterizes the Sami,' he wrote in his book."

"Go on, Henrik, you were going to tell them!"

David stiffened. The conversation was threatening to turn to long-winded bear stories. But Vuori seemed not to hear her. He poured out a drink for himself and drank a toast to the mountaineers.

"Kitchen bench for you tonight, Henrik," said Kristina Maria with a smile. "Henrik always has to sleep on the kitchen bench when he's been drinking," she told Torsson.

"Why should I have a man stinking of alcohol beside me?" said Marta, looking sharply at Henrik.

She wanted something. David noticed that the others too were curious. Torsson, on the other hand, was keeping a close eye on how the alcohol was winding its way through David's system.

"Let's go now," he said in an ominous voice, and got up. He took hold of David's arm and pulled him to his feet.

"Nabbed," said David. "David's just beginning to enjoy himself, and now David's got to go home."

"David's enjoyment is too general," said Torsson. "I want him to myself. Besides, he's got to be hung up to dry."

"Henrik!" Marta cried, as if on impulse. "Doesn't it make you sick?"

But Henrik appeared to be in the best of health and didn't answer.

"Eh . . . what?" whispered Eklind, who had only thirty years of Rakisjokk training in controlling his curiosity. Kristina Maria was looking at him through half-closed eyes.

Torsson put his arm through David's and led him out of the school hall, trying to make it look as if he were leaving voluntarily. Marta Vuori came hurrying after them into the yard.

"If Henrik's not going to tell you, then I will."

She seemed slightly intoxicated with her sense of duty, spiced with a satisfactory dose of malice. But Henrik caught up with her and briskly grabbed her arm.

"Off home with you now," he said, more harshly than they'd ever heard him address Marta before.

"Then you tell them."

"There's nothing to tell."

Vuori followed them to Jerf's house all the same. He ran his hand through his hair and swore. "Bloody womenfolk leak like sieves. There's really nothing to tell. But if I'm to tell you, then I want you to promise not to take it seriously."

"Scout's honor," said David. "May I drop dead on the spot if I don't laugh my head off when I hear what you have to tell us."

"Then the outcome will be the same in any case, but I suppose I'll have to take that responsibility."

Torsson unlocked the door and gestured to him to go in. It was rather stuffy and musty inside. Vuori stayed on the steps, twisting his cap.

"No," he said. "Let's cut this crap about womenfolk. I have to tell you I've nothing to tell."

His decisiveness was such that they didn't even bother to call after him as he swept around the corner of the cottage.

"Sure to have been a two-hour bear story," said David, flopping down on the bed with a thud. "He can save it for Christmas." As if hit over the head, David fell fast asleep.

He woke to the sound of low voices. Torsson was hanging out of the window, having a conversation with a low, agitated female voice. Slowly David identified the voice as Marta Vuori's, and in his half-conscious state it held for him all the appeal of a stone crusher.

"I can't take the responsibility, you see."

"No, of course not," said Torsson.

She took a deep breath to provide oxygen for her failing courage. "Henrik says that I mustn't tell you under any circumstances."

"Don't, then," said David from his bed. Torsson surreptitiously aimed a kick at him while his upper and visible half expressed trusting gratitude.

"You won't say anything to Henrik, will you? He'll make my life miserable!"

"We know what a wife batterer he is," David drawled.

Torsson coughed opportunely. "Come on inside," he said, sounding rather like the wolf in Grandmother's nightie.

She entered and looked inquisitively all around the room. David aroused no more interest than the washstand, but he bore that with the same composure as it did.

"Henrik walked past here several times this morning," she began. "And he wondered why you never got up. No one knew anything about this secret expedition of yours, you see."

She paused for a moment to provide a window for the bilateral furnishing of confidences, but no one seized the opportunity.

"In the end he knocked on the door and when no one answered he went in. Tell me . . ." She leaned forward and breathed over Torsson. "Did you have a rope?"

"Rope?" He scratched behind his ear, considering this. "Of course, a rope—yes, we had a rope."

"Well, in that case." She got up impatiently. David, struck by Torsson's resemblance to the wolf in the nightie, said loudly, "Oh, Grandmother, what big ears you've got!"

When no one took any notice, he asked, "What kind of rope?"

"You must know that yourselves," she replied suspiciously. "An ordinary lasso with a noose."

"Aye." Torsson nodded. "Perfectly ordinary. We were going to take it with us."

Marta Vuori was disappointed. But her sense of duty and hope did not abandon her.

"I thought as much," she said. "Henrik said something of the kind, too. But we thought it strange that you should own a lasso. Great subtlety characterizes Stockholmers," she added, and this sudden burst of humor seemed to surprise even herself, for she quickly shut her mouth.

"Is that supposed to be me?" David inquired. He didn't bother to wonder why Torsson was lying about a rope they had never had.

"Aye, hanging the rope up like that. It looked horrible, Henrik said. Don't tell Henrik anything, he'll go mad if he hears he's been deceived."

Even with her quiet laughter, she had an ability to grate on nerves. David followed the direction of her gaze until it fastened on a lamp hook in the ceiling just above his bed.

"Was . . . was it hanging there?"

He had got out of bed and was staring at the hook, his lips trembling slightly.

"You know that," said Torsson, sounding bored.

Marta Vuori was wavering between triumph and disappointment, depending on whom she was looking at. Finally, she swept her shawl more tightly around her and retreated toward the door.

"Wonder where the rope is now?" said Torsson.

"Henrik took it. You want it back, of course? No, don't—I'll be miserable."

"Oh, well, we'll have to put up with the loss."

The door slammed behind her.

"Exit Cassandra," said David. "She'll come back to howl over my grave." They watched her slipping around Jerf's shed and saw her change direction so that she wouldn't be seen coming from their cottage.

"What's up with you?"

Torsson was sitting wild-eyed on a chair, his lips moving. He didn't answer.

"Was it that remarkable?" David asked. "In this series, entitled *Warning Shot*, this evening we heard 'The Rope Trick.' Come on, pull yourself together! Do you really think it was that bad? Someone hung up a rope with a noose above my bed to frighten us. I assure you I'll sleep excellently under that hook."

"It's not that," Torsson mumbled.

"What is it, then?"

But Torsson was sunk deep in thought.

10. YOU DON'T KNOW MATTI

Per-Anti had been staying with his father for a day and a half in the Kaittas tent. The silence from up there was beginning to worry Rakisjokk. Kristina Maria clamped her mouth shut and set about her brother's chores. Occasionally she glanced up toward the forest where the path began but did not confide her fears to anyone.

Early in the morning the day after David and Torsson's

expedition, a sports cap bobbed above the veils of mist by the brewhouse and Per-Anders appeared before Marta Vuori's astonished gaze. He was strangely hunched up and looked anxious in the raw cold. Behind him came a small figure Marta could only with the greatest difficulty recognize. Although there were only two of them, they gave the impression of some kind of procession.

"Herra jumala [Good Lord]!" Marta whispered. "It's Edvin."

She hadn't seen him for a year. He seemed to have shriveled in the winds up there, and he did not so much as glance at her as the two of them walked past. The old man stopped for a long time in front of the shed, gazing at the two reindeer skins stretched out there, thickly plastered with sawdust on the inside. With his finger he pulled a long, greasy tuft of hair out of one of them and shook his head at the premature slaughter that would make them shed more hair than necessary. Otherwise the shooting of the reindeer did not appear to trouble him much.

As they entered the cottage, he kicked at the top step with the curved toe of his boot. Per-Anders flushed because he had failed to mend it. They went into the kitchen and Kristina Maria seemed to be struck more by terror than love of her father, which amused the old man a little, but no more than that; he soon forgot her. Things were as usual. Kristina Maria clamped her mouth shut again and turned back to the stove.

"Would you like some coffee, Father?" she asked redundantly.

Per-Anders had to push her over to the coffee tin to get her to do something. Edvin ran his hand over a chair, then sat down on it. He looked thoughtfully from the radio to the kitchen clock and the flypaper. The first-named was emitting a morning sermon through a whole lot of crackles and growls, the second was ticking away the stony seconds, and the third was torturing the life out of some flies with adhesive and arsenic. Edvin did not look as if he were congratulating humanity on these manifestations of progress.

Despite the early hour, through the agency of Marta, in a few minutes the village was aflame with the news of Edvin's arrival. Eklind was the first to appear at the Jerfs' house. The old man shook with the same silent laughter as the very first time Eklind had landed on the jetty in a fine felt hat and topcoat with a velvet collar. He never tired of Eklind. But apart from that, the old man had not only been changed by his long spell of solitude, they noticed; he was also strangely low-spirited that day, a look of anxiety in his eyes. But he made no mention of the reason for his visit until they were all assembled.

Henrik Vuori sent the eldest further-education student with the *Hork* to Orjas and went in to exchange snuff and experiences with Edvin. Marta was with him but stayed in a corner. Edvin had met her only once, at her wedding feast the year before, and he regarded her as misfortune incarnate, striding on her long legs down into the village and staying. Erik Sjögren often visited Kaittas and entertained Edvin with muddled plans for new kinds of apparatus to forecast the weather. Although the old man could perfectly well feel in his knees and toes which way the weather was veering, he used to listen with a certain amusement to Erik holding forth. Now he lengthily and measuredly shook Erik's hand and invited him to sit down beside him.

Last of all came Anna Ryd. She sat down with her back

156

close to the stove to get warm. A thinning of the air prevailed between her and Kristina Maria, making them both
feel breathless. Henrik Vuori shifted uneasily closer to
them, noting that Kristina Maria's hands, busy with the
coffee, were trembling uncertainly.

Edvin gave a small cough and started to speak in his
carefully formed sentences. Actually, no one had ever
heard him make such a long statement before. He had
come to the village, he said, in order once and for all to
bring to the light of day things he had long concealed. Per-
Anders and the arrival of the Swedish police had made
him realize that his continued silence was not doing any
good. Edvin interrupted himself there, coughing and sliding into a sidetrack that finally led to the conclusion,
astonishing to them all, that he, Edvin, had been guilty of
something quite outside the law.

Edvin stopped at that and sat there with limp hands,
gazing out of the window. They all thought the old man
had been overcome with regret and remorse. With some
emotion, Eklind blew his nose into a blue checked handkerchief. But the old man's steady gaze eventually became
so disturbingly intent that they turned to see what he was
looking at. A face was pressed against the gleaming
kitchen windowpane, the blue eyes wide open, the nose
squashed flat and white against the glass.

"Shoo!" cried Marta Vuori, flapping her hands in front
of her.

A strained and unctuous ear-to-ear smile on the face
outside became the crowning glory of this acrobatic number. Then the hands on the windowsill let go and they
heard a thud as the vision disappeared.

Edvin licked his lips and went over to speaking
Finnish.

Torsson was lying on his bed, looking as if he were beholding spirits in the bottom of his empty coffee cup. He didn't think there was any point in getting up.

"They were sitting around the old man, blinking like a gathering of snowy owls," David reported. "I could swear that was no old bear story he was telling them. Anna Ryd looked as if the sky were about to fall on her, and Eklind was almost in tears. Do something! We can't just sit here waiting for them to come and confide in us."

"Huh," said Torsson. "Sooner or later we'll find out what it is. If only we had a newspaper from Stockholm, fresh off the press," he went on dreamily, sunk in a vision of newsagents, coffee shops with jukeboxes playing "Angelique," and long queues for the cinema.

"When you say a newspaper from Stockholm, you mean the day-old one you get in town. You don't know what a paper fresh off the press is."

"Nor do you," said Torsson. "You've never been up that early."

David devoted himself to an April issue of the *Ladies' Journal* and said nothing. Occasionally he checked through the window that the convention at the Jerfs' was still going on. No one emerged from the other end of the cottage. The smoke from the chimney sometimes descended in a fierce gust from the lake, testifying that the inhabitants of Rakisjokk were blending confessions with coffee and would continue to do so for some time.

Not until about eight o'clock did the door creak and Sjögren emerge as the first to leave this meeting. He wore an expression of extraordinarily deep thought.

"Bloody hell, he actually looks quite intellectual," said David. "Look, here comes Eklind. He's weeping. He's on his second handkerchief, I might add."

One by one, they came out and sloped off home. No one seemed about to make any confession. After yet another moment or two, old man Jerf came out into the yard with Per-Anders. They were carrying birch-bark backpacks and rucksacks and they vanished into the shed. Henrik Vuori and Sjögren joined them, similarly equipped, and soon they had dragged out various poles, ropes, and spades from the shed and shared the load out between them. Per-Anders had a lasso over his shoulder. Sjögren had rolled up a tarpaulin and a tent canvas, and a silent Vuori helped him strap it on his back. After shuffling his feet in the doorway for a while, David timidly approached the company by the shed and politely asked if he could help in any way. No one even laughed at him; no one answered.

"Are you off on an excursion?" he asked ingratiatingly. At that, old man Jerf started flapping his hands as if David were a fly. David retreated with dignity and asked Torsson to go out and have a try.

"Let them go," said Torsson indolently, turning over. "They'll be back."

They set off in a body and all David could ascertain was that they were not heading for Kaittas. Kristina Maria was standing on the steps of their cottage with her hands under her apron, watching them until they looked like ants on the reddish-brown slope. A buzzard screeching in the empty sky tempted Vuori's dog into barking, and that was the last they heard of them.

———

It started to rain toward noon. Cold and insistent, the drizzle soaked the jagged leaves of the dwarf birches and pricked the pewter-gray surface of the lake with a million pins. There was no sign of those who remained in Rakis-jokk. An abandoned bunch of tourists who had come on the morning boat were wandering around looking lost in the cold and damp, scanning the skies for the beauty of the mountains. But in vain. Rakisjokk might just as well have been at the bottom of a hole sealed at the top with damp wadding. All they could see of life in the wide-open spaces was David in the window, wrapped in a plaid blanket, solving the crossword in the *Ladies' Journal*. Even before one o'clock they had taken their seats under the tarpaulins on the *Hork* and were waiting for the boy to take them back.

"Poor things!" said one lady with conviction as the *Hork* at last cast off. "Did you see that fat man in the loud shirt? He looked quite timorous."

"No wonder."

The tourists sighed with satisfaction as the village grew grayer and smaller in the mist, finally to merge with the clouds and disappear like something they had seen in a confused morning dream.

The boy at the wheel had orders to blame the weather—even if the sun had been blazing in the sky—and not bring any more tourists over to the village that day. As things were, he didn't have to refuse anyone. Anna Salminen's jetty was totally deserted. So the boy played at being a racing driver on the way back as long as the *Hork* obliged, and returned to Rakisjokk frozen and soaking wet. It occurred to him that he was on his own now, but he couldn't be bothered to wonder why the men had given him that instruction.

In the middle of the day they became visible on the mountainside. They looked tired, dragging their feet and often stopping to rest. David had rushed to the window when he heard dogs barking, at first thinking someone was hurt. But then he counted them and found that they were four, just as when they started out.

But between them they carried a long, awkward construction of poles and canvas, lashed like a Sami sledge and securely tied to each carrying pole. Once down in the village with their burden, they were met by Eklind from the schoolhouse. He stood in their way with his head bowed. They walked past David and Torsson without speaking. Sjögren was the first to go to the shed and open the door. The men had some trouble getting the long stretcher inside. When they came out again, they put their caps back on and disappeared in to Kristina Maria. Only old man Jerf hesitated outside the shed door. Then he came over to Torsson and for a long time stood there running his hand over his cap.

"Aili's come home now," he said finally.

Torsson moved to catch him, as he seemed about to faint, but he recovered and slowly straightened up. His back was trembling under Torsson's hands.

"Jerf, you've got to tell us about it now," Torsson said in a low voice, taking the old man's arm and ushering him into the warmth of the kitchen.

"He hasn't got the strength," said Per-Anders.

The men were silent. Beads of sweat had formed on their foreheads, but nonetheless they were shivering in their wet jackets. Kristina Maria was busy with her inevitable coffee. She showed no trace of tears, but her eyes were rigid, as if she'd seen some horror. She didn't dare glance at her father and jumped whenever she heard him speak. Torsson sat down among them on a kitchen chair and said nothing for a long spell. Finally he started speaking, very quietly.

"I realize you've all had as much as you can take for today," he said, "and I'm not going to rush you. But I have to phone through to town soon, and it would be good if you could tell me where you've come from with . . ." He swallowed and gestured with his head toward the shed.

Sjögren said the long place name with no difficulty.

"Oh, aye," said Torsson, "we've been there too. There's a *passesadje* there from the old days . . . it was no place for us."

Edvin Jerf's eyes glinted.

"We had bad weather," Torsson went on, "so we had to leave."

"You knew, then?" Per-Anders asked hesitantly.

"Not for sure, but we had some idea."

"I have done wrong," said Edvin suddenly. "My mind couldn't cope with what happened to Aili."

As always, silence fell whenever he spoke. After a while Per-Anders said hurriedly, almost excitedly, "Father has done no wrong. Everything he did, he did for Aili's sake and it would have been better if it could have stayed that way. But when Father told me the other day what happened a year ago, I realized that we had to make sure you learned the truth. Otherwise you would probably have found out by yourselves. Father acted the way we did in the old days . . . before the town came and police and all that . . . there was no harm in it."

Almost out of breath, he concluded his long statement. His eyes turned away from his father's and he gratefully slurped the hot coffee his sister handed him. When he had put the cup down, there was silence in the cottage for a moment, but suddenly Edvin snapped, his eyes flashing:

"Stop that damned clock, will you, so I don't have to hear that eternal—"

Kristina Maria leaped up on a chair with fright and seized the pendulum.

The silence did not seem liberating to Torsson. "If you could bear to tell me now," he asked gently.

"Father isn't up to telling it all over again," said Per-Anders. "But I'll do it."

He took his father's arm and spoke quietly to him in Sami. Together they went over to the parlor door.

"No, I think I'd rather go back up to Kaittas," the old man suddenly said in Swedish, trying to free himself. He was breathing quickly.

"Oh, don't!"

Kristina Maria clapped her hand to her mouth at the same moment as she contradicted her father for the first time in her life. Per-Anders came to her aid.

"I think she's right, Father. You'd suffer in this weather. We've had a hard day. It would please me greatly," he said formally, "if you would stay, Father."

The old man went slowly into the parlor and closed the door behind him.

"My sister Aili," said Per-Anders, pressing his hands to his temples, "took her own life."

The words hung in the clockless air. Torsson nodded quietly.

"It was in July last year, and Father buried her up there."

Per-Anders began to cry, a man's harrowing deep sobs tearing at his lungs, and was unable to go on. Between gulps of air, he asked Henrik Vuori to take up the story. Henrik spoke as quietly as he could, turning away from the parlor door and Per-Anders. With some difficulty, Torsson managed to catch what he was saying.

"Edvin told us this morning when he arrived. He asked us to go up with him and help bring down her body. She had hanged herself in a lasso. This was high up in the mountain in a camp quite near that valley. An old summer camp for the Karesuando Sami who used to pass through there. She was inside an empty tent, so no one found her at first, when we were all out looking for her. Edvin decided to say nothing and bury her quietly up there . . . for her own sake."

"But why?"

"Well, I suppose he didn't want the others to know what had happened to her."

"But why did she do it?"

Henrik looked at Per-Anders first for his agreement before he said it.

"She needed to marry," he said, and at first Torsson didn't understand.

"A baby?"

"Aye, she was expecting one. But no one wanted to take the responsibility."

David had been sitting very quietly on the firewood box all this time. Now the scene in front of him suddenly blurred. A kind of mist appeared before his eyes, and he had understood the situation long before Henrik spoke the final words:

"It was Matti's."

As if through running water, he heard voices and almost forgotten remarks, Anna Ryd's flinty words on the way to Orjas, when he had said that Matti had loved life: "Not all life."

Then he remembered Per-Anders with a cold glint in his eye up there at Kaittas the day before yesterday: "You didn't know Matti."

No, he hadn't known Matti. You don't get to know each other over a Stockholm winter. They had all thought Aili was the love of his life. Love—he tested the word and it was weightless. And yet there was something about Matti that meant that David wished he had taken that advice and not looked into all this. Who had really benefited now? Not Aili.

He felt an arm around his shoulder and thought it was Torsson, but when he looked up, it was Per-Anders leaning over him, mumbling something he at first didn't understand.

"He was a friend of yours, I know. That's the way it is. There, now, let's go easy."

David didn't know where Per-Anders found the strength for this.

"And Matti?" Torsson inquired quietly.

"Perhaps we shouldn't think too badly of him," said Henrik. "Perhaps he never even knew. Aili wasn't like other women."

But David noticed that not one of them believed him, not even he himself.

"He was up at Kaittas in March, and after saying nothing all that time, Edvin talked. So what happened was that Matti went out into the snow. You can understand that."

"Aye," said Torsson, "you can."

"As for him not knowing," said Henrik, "of course he knew. But he probably thought she got lost on the mountain. It was too much for him when he was told she'd taken her own life because of him."

Torsson rose stiffly—he had been sitting very still on his chair—and went over to the door.

"I'd better have a look before I phone," he muttered to Sjögren, who was sitting nearest the door. Together they went out to the shed. David followed them to the door and watched Torsson going cap in hand into the gloom.

Inside was a stillness that made Torsson remember the howling of the wind through the cracks in March. Now the light was glinting through them, creating a pattern of stripes on the tarpaulin. While Sjögren fiddled with ropes and tight knots, Torsson found himself listening to a bird singing in a birch outside.

David saw Torsson coming out with an expression of great weariness on his face. His eyes had disappeared and he kept rubbing his forehead without noticing he was doing it.

"Are you going to phone?"

"Aye. But first I've got to ask Edvin something. It can't be helped. Poor man!"

He went back into the house and David followed. Inside, none of them had stirred from their chairs. To David, they seemed to have petrified into a picture and would never be able to move again. Kristina Maria didn't even turn around from her place by the stove as they walked past.

"Per-Anti, do you think I could have a word with your father?"

"Oh, all right."

Torsson knocked on the parlor door and went in. The

room was small and furnished with dark, solid oak pieces. A small organ stood by the window, a reminder of the days when the preacher used to come on his rounds and hold services. Edvin Jerf was sitting on a small stool as if asleep with his eyes open, his fingers fumbling with the belt around his waist, fingering and fingering as if searching with vacant eyes for something.

"Terve," Torsson mumbled in greeting, affected by the proximity of the organ and the solemn pictures on the walls. "I'm sure you're tired and would prefer to be left in peace."

"Everything must come out," the old man said quietly.

David noticed he had no trouble speaking Swedish now. Everything seemed to have become a matter of indifference to him.

"I've learned what happened from Per-Anders and Henrik," said Torsson. "But there's something I'd like you to tell me."

Edvin nodded.

"How come you finally talked to Matti? He knew nothing—or at least not everything—until he went up to Kaittas in March."

Edvin appeared to find it difficult to follow what the policeman was saying. Was it one question or several?

"Knew about . . . he knew all right. When someone's going to be a father, he knows it."

"Aye, but that she . . . that she didn't get lost. Did he know that?"

"I don't know."

He looked coldly at David, as if the similarity between him and Matti had just occurred to him for the first time.

"Clocks, clocks!" he mumbled fiercely.

For a moment David thought the old man had become

confused with grief and emotion, but then he suddenly realized that Edvin was listening to the faint ticking of the wristwatch he had for some reason put on. Edvin was longing for Kaittas and silence. David couldn't stop his watch. All he could think of was to turn it around so that it faced his wrist and they didn't have to see the fine second hand racing around.

"Aye, he came up occasionally," Edvin went on, his voice steadier now. "He'd bring coffee and other things I needed from time to time. Sometimes other people came, sometimes it was him. I thought quite a bit, certainly, but I never got around to saying anything. He found out by himself."

"Matti? Was he at Kuott . . . kuo . . . ?"

"Oh, no." Despite everything, Edvin smiled. "Not in March. No one goes there then. I told him."

He suddenly put his fragile, bird-boned hand on top of David's asking, "You were his friend?"

David nodded.

"Then let me tell you . . . maybe he didn't know what had happened to Aili after all. But he must have known about the other thing. A person would know. Still, he probably thought she'd got lost. But then he saw my bark knapsack. He opened it before I had time to stop him . . . he wanted to borrow it, I think. And there were her ornaments and the lasso. He recognised the ornaments, of course. So I had to tell him."

"Where's the knapsack now?"

"He took it. He wouldn't listen." Edvin blinked in the light from the windows and turned away from them. "I would've liked to keep those ornaments," he mumbled. "On my own, I went up there to fetch them several days later."

11. ONLY THE DRAGONS KEEP SILENT

They were living in a cauldron whose sides were mountains, and occasionally it amused someone to stir with a ladle down there where the steamy cloud was thickest, changing the weather within hours. On a day like this, the cold and the fine drizzle had seemed appropriate. But the one with the ladle thought differently. Now heat came creeping along the edges of the cauldron. Considering that the police would be coming—in their own boat from Orjas—this all-revealing sun was embarrassing. With sarcastic malice it made everything sparkle: weathered house timbers and the holes left by blown-down tiles as well as bleary eyes and faded anoraks. Vuori's dog scratched its coat in the small area of shade from the Jerfs' shed, but was kicked and sworn at so that even the fleas stopped short.

Rakisjokk walked in shame and anguish. It hardly occurred to anyone that only Edvin Jerf might be treated roughly by the police because of Aili's disappearance; they had a feeling that all of them would be held responsible. First it would come out how they had deceived the police in the question of where and when Matti had died. And now this. The only person to attempt a joke was Erik Sjögren, who felt released from his private anguish in this collective anxiety. He presumed that either they would all be locked up or the town would allot them a policeman to patrol Rakisjokk's jetty and supervise them both winter and summer. He only hoped it would be Torsson.

Torsson was packing. The remainder of his holidays would still run to a trip to Eskilstuna. He imagined himself sitting in the park below Carl Milles's sculpture of the Hand of God with a fruit drink (no more coffee for him), eating almond cakes and watching the ducks bobbing along on the green water.

David couldn't bring himself to pack. He had only thirty kronor, not even enough for petrol to Svappavaara.

"Now," said Torsson. "I'm ready. We've just got to get hold of that bark bag before the boat comes with the others."

"Where is it?"

"Well, Anna had it."

"Don't you think she's got rid of it?"

He didn't think so. You couldn't move in Rakisjokk without being observed, and her eyes had had that broody-hen look in them until this very day. But if she had laid that egg somewhere, then she knew where it was and now she had nothing to hide.

"You can go and get it, for that matter," said Torsson, a glint in his eye. "Listen to what she has to say. I'm curious to see how your love affair develops."

David sloped off with a bad taste in his mouth. The upstairs window of the headmaster's house had a roller blind and he knew she was entrenched behind it. Was she packing, too?

No, she was sitting upright at her desk, her hands clasped on the green blotter. Her desk calendar had stopped at March, and he realized that no time had passed for her since then. Out of habit or indifference, she turned her fine profile to him, though it had grown thinner and her nose looked a little sharp in the harsh light.

"Are you satisfied now?"

She maintained her habit of not looking at the person she was talking to.

"Yes, of course. Fancy you getting to know me so well in this short time."

It struck him that she was capable of very enduring love. On a whim, Matti had dragged her with him up here from Stockholm, then forgotten her and treated her as if she had always been there, meanwhile ruining another woman and causing her death. But Anna was still prepared to try to conceal his activities from anyone wanting to poke his nose into them. How much pain had Matti inflicted on her? David didn't want to know the answer to that question. Despite everything, she was still the girl with hard eyes who had told him Matti was dead.

"I want the bark knapsack," he said abruptly.

She got up and went into a closet, then rummaged around in there among suitcases and books. She must have hidden it well. When she emerged from the dark, she was dragging a large rucksack, and he surprised himself by not making any attempt to help her. She undid the leather straps and pulled out the bark bag.

"There you are."

He ran his fingers over it, then put it on a chair by the door.

"Leave this place," he said, his voice sharper than he had intended.

She looked up with an amused glint in her eye. "Your concern is touching. I think you should leave this place yourself."

"What else is new?"

He realized this conversation would go on forever in these short jabs if he didn't do something about it. She had returned to her place at the desk and clasped her hands in front of her.

"Would you mind telling me how you got the bag?"

"The same day I met you for the first time," she replied flatly. "But I'd had it all spring without knowing it."

Noticing that she wanted to unburden herself on this subject, he was careful not to move in the chair.

"Matti came down from Kaittas that Saturday afternoon in March. He came up to me and behaved extremely oddly. He had the birch-bark bag with him, but I didn't think much about it. He seemed confused, as if he had been hit by something. I went down for a few minutes to make some coffee for him . . ."

This eternal coffee, David thought. The whole of Rakisjokk is nothing but one long caffeine poisoning.

". . . but when I came back upstairs, he'd gone. Well, I was used to that."

She pursed her lips and glanced at him.

"Then in July, that day when we met, I was going to pack my things to go south. I found the bag hidden right at the back of the closet under a whole lot of summer clothes Matti knew I wouldn't touch. I suppose he didn't dare take it back to his place, and perhaps he thought he'd pick it up later. I was . . ."

She fell silent, then noticed him again. She didn't want to confide all that much in him, after all.

"You thought he'd killed Aili?"

"Yes."

No hesitation at all.

"Why?"

"I had some idea she was pregnant."

It takes time, David reflected, before you get used to thinking so harshly. But she had had plenty of time up here.

"So I went off with the bag in a state of panic. I intended to get shot of it. I didn't know what I was doing. But I never managed to dump it. Thanks to you, mostly. Kristina Maria helped you, too. She had an attack of suspicion the other day when you were up in Kaittas, and she nearly drowned me in her eagerness. Then I just about gave up trying to get rid of it. And now it's too late."

"Was there any point in hiding it?"

She turned slowly toward him. He could see what he had not noticed before—that the yellow blouse was grubby around the collar and her nails were bitten down to the quick. When she replied, he realized she was going to stay in Rakisjokk.

"Yes, there was."

He hid the bag under his bed and then went off to find Torsson. The police boat had not yet arrived. Kristina Maria had packed a lunch and a backpack of provisions for Edvin Jerf, and no one thought to prevent him from leaving now that the weather had improved. He had done what he had set out to do, and the police could listen to the others. Torsson did not know he was going, but David stood in the school doorway and watched him disappearing. As soon as he got beyond the brewhouse, he adopted the calm pace he aimed to keep up for the next twenty kilometers. He wasn't going to Kaittas. That now seemed to him too near the village. Twenty kilometers to the south was a summer camp site where he could be sure of being spared frequent visits. Kristina Maria stood in the doorway until he vanished.

David found Torsson in the craft room, where he appeared to be measuring the floor with long, ponderous strides.

"The bag's under my bed if you want it," said David.

"So you've been there?"

"Yes. We exchanged ice-cold looks for five minutes. But Anna Ryd thinks it's more blessed to give than to receive. You know, there's nothing more reliable than real antipathy at first glance—it becomes a kind of tenderness in the end. We dislike each other so much, we slobber with hatred."

"The way you go on," Torsson muttered. "You can certainly talk."

"You're looking very pleased with yourself, for that matter. Are you quite satisfied now? You think you've solved the Rakisjokk mystery, and you're just waiting for the chief of police to come and fasten a medal on your fat chest."

"Well," said Torsson, "I've found out a few things. Undeniably," he added with the shadow of a smile. He sauntered off and opened the door to the school hall.

"You might at least give me my due," said David. "I played a part in it. But I'm not satisfied."

Torsson sighed absent-mindedly and opened the door from the school hall leading out into the classroom corridor at the back of the building.

"Haven't you noticed how this story creaks with improbabilities?"

"No."

It smelled of school corridor out there and David shuddered with painful recollections. "I'm Strindbergian when it comes to memories of school."

"So's everyone," said Torsson with unexpected literary insight, or just intuition.

They could hear Eklind talking about the ice age on the other side of a door. The scraping of feet and rustling noises indicated that his story was not the most sensational the children had ever heard. Torsson opened the door to the backyard and the dustbins and went down the steps. The sun was beating down on the wall where the emergency sledge hung on its hooks.

"Torsson," said David earnestly, "tell me how Matti made his way up to the place where he lay down in the snow, on a pair of skis with bindings too small for his feet."

Torsson was looking along the path that wound its way up the slope, the path Per-Anders had taken on skis the morning he found Matti.

"Oh, that. He was drunk."

"And that makes your feet shrink?"

David tried to catch Torsson's eye, but it was resting on something far away among the birch trees.

"I can go along with that," said David, "if you like. But what about his boots?"

"Oh, that," said Torsson dismissively, "that's nothing to get worked up about. He probably stuck his feet into the skis without fastening the bindings—he wasn't going far. It wouldn't have crossed his mind, wild and crazy as he was. In that state, there are worse things."

"Like what?"

Torsson turned and went back inside. David had to whip around like a dog in his tracks to get in through the doors Torsson kept swinging shut behind him. They returned to the school hall.

"Over there," said Torsson, pointing at the table by the door to the craft room. "That's where Eklind's mah-jongg hand was laid out, waiting for the children to see what a miracle he had achieved. But they never saw the Big Three Dragons. Eight little tiles."

"His hand brushed them. Remember, he'd cut his hand and the green dragon you found was bloodstained."

"That sounds good to me. But . . ." He turned around slowly and laid his hands on David's shoulders, breathing heavily. "I don't understand why he washed them."

Torsson sank into the armchair in front of the fire and stared fish-eyed out over the hall.

"That," he said, "is a superhuman action quite beyond my limited comprehension. I don't know what I'm going to tell the chief when he comes. First of all, Matti was a painter and must have known the colors would run when he washed the tiles. Even if he hadn't thought about it, he would have given up the moment he saw the result of water on the first tile. But evidently it was desperately vital to get that blood off. Why? He'd only cut his hand. Secondly, he was drunk and about to kill himself. Do you think he would start dabbling tiles in water in that state of mind?"

He looked up at David. "Close your mouth. Listen, did Matti play mah-jongg?"

"Aye."

"Don't you start saying aye, too. You might get stuck up here. So he played mah-jongg, did he? Now do you see?"

"What should I see?"

"Visions, presumably, because that's what I'm doing. *Herran täbðen* [Good grief]! What am I going to tell the chief? And what was he doing out there in the school hall? Matron's skis were propped up outside the craft-room steps, I'm told. He didn't have to go through the hall. My head's spinning. Not to mention that rope affair of Marta Vuori's."

"That! Are you still concerned with that? That could have been anyone wanting to scare us away."

"And the shooting of those reindeer? Which I was supposed to investigate. Well, it'll no doubt be a terrible story on the day of reckoning. When the man from the vineyard comes to see how I've carried out my duties."

With that, he opened the door and plodded off away from the school. A dull buzzing noise could be heard from the lake as if a large horsefly were circling toward them in the sun. A reflection flashed in a windshield. The police boat was approaching. The man from the vineyard was on his way.

Hearing the buzzing, Torsson went down to the jetty to stand and await his judge and inquisitor.

Mechanically David glanced up the slope to see whether Jerf had disappeared from sight. The old man deserved to be spared. He had been gone a long time and there was no sign of him any longer. Poor old man, trudging on in this heat.

"On my own, I went back to fetch the ornaments."

The words struck David like a flash of lightning from an empty sky. He realized their importance long before he had grasped the full significance. Once logic began to function, the whole matter was reduced to a suspicion, but the adrenaline had already begun pumping, and he could feel the back of his neck prickling as he stood there, upright in the sun, clenching his fists in his trouser pockets. His first thought was to rush down to Torsson and blurt out what he thought. But when he got there, the police boat had already arrived and Torsson was standing on the jetty with a servile and obtuse expression fixed on his face, offering his arm to help a gray-haired man with braid on his sleeves out of the boat.

"Torsson . . . Torsson, can I have a word with you?" David tugged at Torsson's shirt.

"Get off! If they're to believe that I've still got my wits about me at all, you'd better not show your face," Torsson hissed. Then, his face blank again, he turned to his chief, who was now regarding Rakisjokk with a grimace and sighing as if he had already had enough of it.

"What's this? Rakisjokk? Well, well. Don't forget I've no intention of speaking Finnish. Can you get a cup of coffee here, do you think?"

Another caffeine addict looking for a fix, David thought. Well, you go right ahead. I'm going to get him. He rushed back to their room at the back of the Jerfs' house and took from Torsson's well-packed suitcase the map they had used when they went up the mountain. Grease-spotted interview transcripts scattered over the floor, but David was in too much of a hurry to put them back. He spread the map out on the table where the mah-jongg game was still laid out. The place was called Vassijokk. Twenty kilometers away . . . but the old man couldn't have got there yet. David would have to find paths and follow the route he thought Edvin had taken. And then he'd have to shout. Etvina . . .

He took nothing with him except pipe and tobacco as he hurried off across the yard. The smoke was rising thick and straight out of the Jerf chimney and he cursed the coffee maniacs one last time. He had only reached the osier swamp when he had to slow down and eventually sit down for a while to ease the stitch in his side. He realized he would have to go at the same economical pace as the old man, and he just hoped old Jerf had taken a rest somewhere once he felt he was far enough away from Rakisjokk.

No mosquitoes attacked David in the heat. His skin was covered with a clammy membrane of sweat, and a sour smell came from under his shirt. Strangely enough, the going seemed easier than before, now that he had slowed his pace slightly. He gave a fleeting thought to their experiences the previous day in the *passesadje* valley. Of course the weather might turn nasty again, but there was nothing he could do about that.

He still hadn't started calling out to Edvin. Something held him back. Laboriously, he tried to analyze the feeling that prevented him, but failed. He now knew less than ever about what had really happened in Rakisjokk. But he knew one thing: if he could only get hold of the old man, a lot would be clarified. I must have been in a daze, sitting there on the firewood box in Per-Anti's kitchen, he thought.

The path marked on the map looped down toward lower ground. It looked like an unnecessarily roundabout route, but he now knew quite a lot about marshes and swamps, and about rain-slippery moraine in difficult terrain devoid of chlorophyll. From where he was standing he could see the flashing cats' eyes of two lakes on the bluish plain, and the forest looked like a homespun army with crossbows marching up into the wilderness. The only living things he saw were two reindeer cows veering away in alarm as they caught his scent. He also heard a shrill cry, as cracked as a broken organ pipe, but he did not know that it was the alarm call of a female eagle.

In among those fearful trees, anguish did my marrow freeze—the line of verse came back to him when he entered the spruce forest, where not the slightest breeze moved in their dark green, ragged beards. The path kept branching off into false trails, presumably leading straight to some hell or other. He ought to have brought a compass. He stuck to what he thought was the widest path. Solitary cloudberry flowers glimmered here and there on the barren ground. Without warning, the forest came to an abrupt end, and for a moment he hesitated before stepping out into the heat and the sun-scorched grass.

He had thought he was in a wilderness and his initial reaction when he saw the building, a wooden shack, was fear. He had emerged from a protruding tongue of forest and the last spruces touched the turf roof of the cabin. He backed a little way in among the trees and sat down to look at the map. Sweat dripped on the paper and was quickly absorbed. There was nothing on the map to indicate any habitation here. But when he approached the building again, he saw that a whole village lay huddled on the hillside. He could just see the village street, little more than a cattle track between the cottages, curving away into a dreary bend down toward a glimpse of water between the birches. A well lever pointed to infinity like a knowing finger. Water, he thought, nothing could be better.

With some hesitation — what kind of people lived in a place that was not even on the map? — he went around the first building, a barn, and emerged between the two cottages by the well. They're quiet, anyway, he thought, and they're no coffee addicts. Not the slightest trickle of smoke was rising into the empty sky.

He leaned over the well to arrange a smile of welcome to his own reflection in the water. But no face met his. Way down toward the bottom, a small chickweed wintergreen was living an insecure life in green moss, which was climbing damply up the walls. The scoop lying beside the dried-up well was rusty and crumbling away.

He looked in through the nearest broken window. Slowly the desolation dawned on him. It might have been years since anyone had trodden the track or mentioned the village by name. The cottages were derelict and a winter storm had already destroyed two of them. Nonetheless, some signs remained of those who had lived there; despite their poverty, they had been able to leave the most worthless things behind. A metal bucket and a broken drop-leaf table could be seen through a window. Blind, black windows gaped. But he sensed that no curtains had ever hung there—the puritanical severity of everything that met his eye told him that at one time pious and hard-working members of a Protestant sect had lived here. Frivolity had crept into the cottages now that no one any longer paid heed to the racing winds or swept the steps—a pink willow herb had forced its way up between two floorboards and was sinfully flowering in a ray of sunlight from the door.

Profound silence makes the ears as sensitive as a fox's. David froze when he heard a faint creak, as if someone had trodden too heavily on a rotten step. Then he heard footsteps, soft and heavy at the same time, coming along the track. He licked his dry lips and refrained from calling out. The footsteps out there sounded nothing like dry little Edvin's.

12. ON MY OWN, I WENT . . .

I woke in the middle of the night. I remember opening my eyes and staring straight out into the dark. Is he still alive? I thought.

I lay there listening. The night was a thousand kilometers deep all around us. Then I heard the cold snapping like shots in the walls. I sank back against the pillow. No, he couldn't be alive. I licked my chapped lips and tried to go back to sleep.

I still occasionally wake in the middle of the night. Or am I dreaming? It's dark all around me and I lie turning the idea over. Could he still be alive? How many hours have passed? Does it take a long time to die that way? My blood seems to be flowing as turgidly as lead and I have to drag myself up through the nightmare to open my eyes at last and see that the room is full of the white light of a summer night. He's been dead a long time.

You throw a stone into the water and the circles spread. Sooner or later those watered circles will cease and the surface must close over its secret. I wish it were so. But it's as if bewitched . . . ever more circles.

Into what kind of witchy water have I thrown my stone? Have I done anything other than what was necessary?

Today they say in the village that we ought to feel shame and regret for our lies. Well, those who have no more circles to count can afford to say that. I have to go through it all over and over again to check whether I've forgotten anything. I'm sure they're capable of making out that I was the one who held the lasso and that it flew hissing through the air and settled around Aili's neck. As the one who found her, I'm the only one who knows that she herself took it with her when she disappeared. Although my words may have been ringing in her ears, it was her own hands that made the noose in the lasso and fastened the end to the vent at the top.

I must have been another person that time when I crept into the empty summer tent and saw her feet in the air. I felt relief—I could hardly have felt anything else. But I knew at once what I would do and I was aware of my influence over Edvin. Confused with grief and shame as he was, he did everything I told him. My fear did not make itself felt until we were burying her over there in the valley of the shamans. That place gives you the feeling that eyes are watching you, doesn't it?

Today we have this bloody sun, damn it. I think every single blade of grass in Rakisjokk is outlined as if by a searchlight. There must be things I've never considered. What might not enter the minds of those policemen? In the darkness last winter, everything was fine. I could sit and think of tons of snow on top of that haunt of shamans. Snow, silence, and forgiving darkness.

Forgiving? No, grinning darkness. No doubt you can deceive yourself with that kind of winter darkness and think it will last forever. But for half the year, the scoop of the sky opens up and freezes us with its light. Are you hiding something? the sun says, tormenting us.

There goes that artist; he's grinning, too, his eyes racing around like ball lightning in his head. He came here with tears in his eyes for his friend Matti. God knows, he may have to forget it all. But even the crassest idiot may stumble on something, something I've forgotten.

Edvin is a person who can keep his mouth shut. I was sure he would go on saying nothing for the rest of his life—he can't have much longer to go, either. But when Matti came down from Kaittas in March, I knew the old man had talked. But why? He came into the kitchen where we were sitting with a look in his eyes like some poor dog that's caught the scent of a wolverine. The moment he spoke, I saw that his eyes were seeking mine. He needn't have used that oracular language—I already knew. As soon as he began to rave about going to town, I was frightened. But I also knew he was now afraid of me.

He wouldn't dare say anything as long as he didn't have Rakisjokk behind him. He was intending to go to the police, I realized that. When I went into the craft room, he was still lying face down over that picture of his. I thought he was dead and the relief that came over me made me start sobbing like a child.

But I managed to pull myself together sufficiently to unbutton his jacket and feel his heart. He was still alive, all right. I saw the knife lying there, and his bloodstained hand. It would have been easy at that moment to finish it off. But I could never have done that.

I carried him carefully away, out through the school hall. It was when we were passing the door and the table inside it that the nightmare began. That's just the kind of thing you dream about toward morning when you've been lying awkwardly on your back. His hand swung out as I turned to get him through the door and every single one of those stupid little mah-jongg tiles went flying to the floor. I froze. Had the noise woken the children upstairs? But the house was quiet. I shoved the tiles under the table with my foot. Lying on the cold floor, Matti started snoring, or breathing roughly, and I realized I had to hurry.

I got him out through the school corridor, and by then the cold was already considerable, though it was still snowing. I hoped for more snow, so the sledge tracks wouldn't show. As if he were a child, I packed him down into the sledge I'd taken down from the wall. Even today I can't understand why I laced him into it so thoroughly. I had trouble with the ropes when I got up the hill with him.

It was heavy going up the steep rise. Every second, I was afraid he would regain consciousness. But I thought of all the alcohol he'd drunk. And if he woke, I could say I'd found him up there. I kept turning around, trying to distinguish the village in the dark. For a long time I could see the light shining above the steps to the craft room. Actually, those were my worst moments, when I fetched the skis in the glare of that light and laid them over the sledge. The skis kept sliding off. That was another part of the nightmare, which made me curse and sob in the darkness.

When I at last got him up there and out of the sledge, I was so exhausted, I just wanted to get it over with. Before leaving, I don't think I even glanced at him once I had laid him down in the snow. But I could hear his jagged breathing. I regretted afterward not having fastened the skis on his feet.

In the school hall, those mah-jongg tiles were still lying under the table. I had to do something about them. They had blood spattered all over them. You'd think it was only in my nightmares that a single sweep of a lifeless hand can stain every one of them with blood. If people realized Matti had been in the school hall, then they would start wondering. The only way to reach the sledge without being seen was through there, and that shouldn't be hard to work out. It was important not to lead anyone's thoughts to the sledge. Maybe I was too calculating? But those tiles frightened me.

I set about trying to wash them. The water running into the zinc bowl in the kitchen made an awful racket. How was I to know the colors would wash off? The water turned red and green, and the colors went on running over the white bone surfaces. It was impossible to get it off altogether. Those red incisions might have been wounds bleeding in the water. But I managed to get the real blood off. I couldn't leave the tiles lying there crying out that someone had been there trying to clean them that same night, so I put them back in the box and mixed them up with the others. Had that taken hours? I didn't know. Maybe I had already been missed. All I can remember was how tired I was when I finally got to bed, without a single thought in my head.

In the middle of the night, I'm wide awake. Does it take a long time? Mercifully, the cold clamps one's jaws shut with a snap out there. He can't be alive any longer.

The next morning I was tense and practiced expressing consternation with my frozen facial muscles at least ten times. But I had no use for my consternation. He was not found. No one went to look for him, either, and I wasn't going to suggest anything. They seemed to have taken seriously what he said about intending to go into town. Whether you went by day or by night hardly made any difference in that darkness. Matti was not one to lose his way. But they were waiting to hear from him. I don't know, in the end I almost persuaded myself that he was in town in a warm room, laughing at us poor rats in our dark hole. I tried to see something across the lake and seemed to see headlights glinting. Perhaps he had got up out of the snow and cold up there and made his way to town. Perhaps he had been conscious all the time I was carrying him and hauling him along in the sledge.

Their spirits clouded over when we found him. They had liked Matti all right, but what really bothered them was that no one had gone to look for him. What would the police say? I was cautious, as cautious as a dog with tender paws, when I started bringing the possibility of deception into the conversation. It didn't make any difference to Matti, after all. We could say that he hadn't disappeared until the Monday evening. Then we could also maintain that he had been lying at the foot of the school steps, and no one need know anything else. This spread like soothing oil across their sore consciences. I had to go away and hide my face and my near-hysterical laughter when they all agreed. In the end I think each of them persuaded themselves he or she had thought up the idea. Now no one would give a thought to the sledge or those damned tiles, which sooner or later there would be a fuss about. Now he had been lying outside the door all the time.

I was also much calmed when I saw the policeman. He didn't look like a thinker. But he came back, and at once found the person who seemed to find it easiest to talk. The shooting of the reindeer didn't frighten him off. Yet there was some point to it. The wretched business with the rope was worse. I feel ill at the very thought of it. I must have been dizzy with fear; I nearly stepped straight into a black hole.

My worst moment came in the kitchen this morning. When Edvin came down from Kaittas with his priestly expression and the attitude that now everything that had been hidden was to be brought into the light, it made my head swim. What all had the old man been thinking about, sitting up there in that smoky tent? And what had Matti said to him earlier? But the acrid smoke must have penetrated into the old man's brain, because he hadn't been thinking anything at all. He stuck to the subject. I felt as if I were on a sliding glacier while Edvin was talking, and I knew that one stray word could send me dancing down a crack.

What happens is that once more these good-natured creatures feel that they are being weighed down to the ground with collective guilt. They all think they were party to Edvin's crazy stunt. Everyone except the big policeman, of course, and his companion, who most of all resembles a city dog barking and sniffing and running around quite aimlessly. God knows what the policeman thinks behind those slits of eyes, but I don't suppose it's anything very deep.

"Who helped you cut down Aili and who carried her to the valley?"

I thought the moment had come when the policeman and that other bloke went into the parlor. I was minded to leave then. But I stayed to listen, my head aching. Nothing could be heard from inside, except finally Edvin's voice. It was dry and made a sound like reindeer hooves.

"On my own, I went up there to fetch them several days later."

On my own, I went . . . oh, did you hear? No. With the same good-natured expressions, they came out of the parlor. At that moment, I knew that was the last word Edvin was to say on the matter. He must not say anything more.

The police boat has presumably arrived by now. Will they ask about me? Well, there's no going back. The heat seems to have forced everyone to a full stop, for or against. The mind keeps quietly simmering one thought. At one time I thought I had lost track of Edvin, or that he had begun to take roundabout routes on his way to Vassijokk. Not once had I even caught a glimpse of his old leather cap above the birches. It was good to get into the forest. The horseflies don't venture in there and I no longer feel mosquito bites.

Suppose Edvin were to catch sight of me first and step out quite close to me—would he understand?

"Are you following me?"

"Aye."

I'm afraid of Edvin.

"*Mitä sinä sitten tahdot?* [What do you want]?"

What can you answer?

"What I want? I want . . ."

"*Mitä?*"

There are four notches for wolves on the gun.

If Edvin holds out his hand, I'll put the gun into it.

Never. What an idea! How can I be afraid? To begin with, I'll creep up on Edvin without being seen. It's a miracle no one saw me taking the gun down off the wall.

The forest ends here, and beyond, in the heat, the horseflies hover with their engines running. What is that glinting down there?

Oh, what's the matter with me? Didn't I just sink like a stone into the moss so clumsily that I jabbed the butt into my stomach? There's no one here. This must be Poropirtti village, no one has lived here for twenty years. And yet I'm reluctant to approach the cottage walls baking in the sun. The village lies in a depression. If Edvin has already passed it, he'll be up the slope on the other side, able to see right down the village road. I daren't go through without looking around. He would see the glint of the gun barrel in the sun. If I make my way up the other side and stay behind the birches, I'll be able to see whether he's down there. He can hardly have gone much farther and he must be hungry by now, too.

The heather crackles under my feet as I walk. It's so dry, it would only take an oath to set it alight and start a forest fire. But now I have a view of the buildings down there. What a miserable, crooked little street! Nothing but a cattle track, of course. The route taken by the cows determined where the houses would be built. I bet they ended up eating each other here in their poverty. And when the preacher ground their souls to ashes, sulphurous fumes must have come out of the doors.

Something glimmering there. It's a door and some steps. It's Edvin.

He's sitting very still. Edvin is sitting on the steps and has opened his packed lunch. Are his eyes roaming around? Oh, no, I'd better crouch down. Perhaps he'll spot the gun barrel and start calling out? What shall I answer? I can shoot from this distance. But what if I miss? Or just maim him so that he crawls behind the wall? Then I'll have to go down there and over to him. Perhaps his eyes will be open.

"Well, are you coming?"

"Aye."

It would be difficult.

"Mitä sinä sitten tahdot?"

"What I want . . ."

Has he nearly finished down there? Slowly, slowly, I'll have to make my way down through the heather. Now I can't see him any longer. Sweat is running into my eyes. This bloody heat! There's a well lever sticking up against the sun over there. Afterward, I'll have a drink of water.

Here I can stand up straight and walk. Everything is crackling and snapping under my feet. They haven't had any rain up here. Maybe not for weeks. For that matter, there's no one here. A cabin wall has cracked and fallen over there. They had newspaper stuck to the wall, I see. The preacher would have had something to say about that. Strange how clearly I can see everything. If it weren't for the sweat in my eyes. I'll get a drink of water afterward.

As I lean toward the first wall and make my breathing calm and silent, I can see right up the mountain and for a moment believe I'm somewhere else. The snow looks so sparklingly white up there on the ridge. But I know it's several years old, dirty and coarse-grained snow, no good even to melt down for water. At this distance, everything becomes beautiful and remote.

Not a sound from the village path. Edvin is probably sitting there, gazing vacantly, his mind blank. He doesn't mind sitting in the blazing sun. Much has happened to him today. From which direction should I approach? Do I have to be visible at that moment? But perhaps he'll be looking the other way. The main thing is that I make my way with caution.

I step out of the shade. The cattle track winds past me. The flies rise from the wooden wall and swirl around me. The most insolent ones sting my neck and in the middle of the track a horsefly is hovering in the air, perhaps intoxicated by the proximity of body heat for the first time in days. Slowly I wriggle my way around the corner of the cottage, making sure the gun barrel doesn't cast shadows. The sweat running from my temple into the corner of my eye and on down my cheek makes me stop until it has dripped off my face. There's nothing I can do about it.

The light dazzles me when I turn my back to the cottage wall. But there is Edvin.

13. THE SUN NEVER STOPS

David felt he was man enough to control his curiosity. If a taxi had driven up the cattle track in Poropirtti village, he would have been able to persuade himself to get into it and ride away. He took a certain pleasure in letting his thoughts run on such things as taxis, helicopters, and rescue flights while he stood wedged between two shacks listening to the footsteps walking around out there. Lucky

I happened to get in among the houses just at the point where the forest juts out to meet them. At least no one can have seen me, he told himself. He began to feel light-headed from the heat and his quivering nerves. The 64,000-kronor question, he thought.

"Who is coming up the path? You have one minute from . . . now."

But he did not have a minute. Within less than thirty seconds, the perpetrator of those footsteps would be showing his size tens or eight and a halfs in the opening between the two buildings. Try stepping out and yelling "Boo!" and I promise you a shinier medal than Torsson's. With a little gasp, he slipped around the corner of the nearest cottage and sank breathlessly into a bed of fat nettles. The acrid air almost made him cough and not until he managed to suppress the reflex did he realize that he was taking this game of hide-and-seek with depressing seriousness.

He couldn't see the walker—and didn't know whether he really wanted to—but he could see the shadow. It came marching along with a harbinger, a slim streak of shadow sticking straight out of the shadow body. The streak was moving up and down with very small movements. Why was the shadow like a soldier? The answer came as if spoken by someone behind him: Because it's got a gun.

He decided to turn and crawl back to the well and the first barn. Somehow or other, he ought to be able to make his way into the forest and then run. But as he looked back, the grassy slope to the forest lay bathed in light and not even a vole would be able to slink away unseen across it, he reckoned. Instead he began to edge behind the houses away from the path, moving sideways like a crab in the nettles, utterly oblivious of the stings and blisters on his hands and arms. Halfway between two cabins, a considerable distance from the place where the shadow had gone past, he dared move forward to peer out along the track. It was deserted.

The stillness in this Pompeii of the north paralyzed him. His gaze roamed along doors and porch steps and fastened on something familiar—Edvin Jerf's rucksack. The water bottle had fallen over and the contents spilled out on the boards, but the heat was already evaporating all traces of it. Flies were crawling over a half-eaten goat's-cheese sandwich.

He hastily withdrew his head and eased back into the shade behind the corner. The heat out there made his head whirl. He could hear no footsteps. But the silence wasn't total. He could hear a sizzling and buzzing—millions of small, dry lives flickering in the air, apparently excited by the presence of humans. He moved on past a few more cottages. He had the idea of hiding inside one for the time being. He didn't want to get in anyone's way. He would be happy to lie low as long as the shadow soldier did not tire of the monotony of Poropirtti. But sooner or later the coast would have to clear so that he could get back to Rakisjokk and the police.

Dear, kind police, if an idea of what's going on here were to spring up in your coffee-drenched brains, I would spend the rest of my life singing your praises.

He found a weathered door that was slightly ajar. Before venturing out on the sunny side to slip in through the doorway, he decided to take a look through the window to ascertain whether the rats had left any standing room for him. He put his feet on a rusty metal drum on the steep grassy bank below the window and heaved himself up to

196

the pane. Strangely enough, the glass had withstood the storms of twenty winters. It had little bubbles like the cheapest bottle glass and at first he could scarcely distinguish a thing in the murk inside.

Nothing is enhanced by being viewed through greenish glass. But the sight of Edvin Jerf with his back to the wall and his feet thrust out in front of him would have made everything go black before David's eyes, glass or no glass. For scarcely more than a second, he stared wide-eyed at the old man's grasshopper-dry body, and yet his face stuck in his mind in every detail—the eyes wide open, the fly sauntering into the corner of his mouth.

David let go of the windowsill. Staggering, he knocked over the metal drum. It rolled noisily along the grass, completing its glorious part in this drama by striking a kettle-drum blow against a stone below the house.

The clatter of metal died away into an abyss of silence. David had stopped breathing. He was hunched down with his hands held out from his body, waiting. Shortly afterward he heard dull thumps on the ground, but this time the footsteps were coming from diagonally behind the houses and were thudding in the short grass. He hurled himself out into the road and ran, dazzled by the sun, into the nearest opening.

It happened to be a barn. The opening had no door and was high up above the ground, but the planking had been broken on both sides so there was scarcely more than a meter of space against the two short walls. He happened to choose the left one and immediately came up against a mass of lumber preventing him from going in any further. With a pitchfork at his back and his right arm wedged into rotting sledge runners, he pressed himself in as far as he could. His left arm and leg still remained level with the opening. He could do nothing about it. The deep shade across the barn and the unsurpassed filth of his linen jacket led him to hope he would merge into his surroundings. But there was no longer any question of moving. He had heard the shadow soldier kick the metal drum and a low curse sputtered into the dry air.

The next moment his pursuer emerged into the road. For a few moments they were so close to each other that David could have whispered and been heard. Recognition did not arouse in him anything more than a faint sensation of things falling into place. For a while, those feet walked around the cabin with the old man inside, then around David's barn. The search is on, David thought. But he was wrong. The bearer of the gun walked calmly up the steps to the cabin closest to the old man's and sat down. The blue steel of the rifle barrel flashed cheerfully in the sun. The waiting began.

David Malm, my funeral speech about you is going to be brief. David collected his wits. You once had a straight flush of spades with the jack on top and that's the only way you have risen above the masses.

He surprised himself by chewing over a regret tougher than the meat from an overenergetic cow. Disregarding what he had previously heard that day about Matti, he had so little feeling for him now that he would not have cared what happened to him if only he could have avoided being where he was. Why, for instance, wasn't it Torsson standing here wedged between pitchfork and sledge runners? And the old man? If the old man had managed to stay alive for an hour or so more, David could have taken the opportunity of escaping while this target shooting was going on.

Was he ashamed? No, I'm crazy about life, he told

himself defensively. Moreover, he was incapable of thinking ahead. The true coward doesn't believe he can die. David was deep down convinced he hadn't drunk the last cup of coffee of his life. What was basically tormenting him was thirst and heat. The sweat was trickling salt and sour down his neck, and he could make no movement to wipe it off. The flies were greedily biting his arms.

He still had his watch on his left wrist and without turning his head he was able to lower his eyes and look at it. But, having reversed the face in Rakisjokk, he was unaware that half an hour had gone by. His mouth was dry. He realized that the figure out there in the sunlight, who must be suffering from the heat and horsefly bites a hundredfold compared with David, had something he did not possess. Patience.

There is infinite patience up here. This is due to time, which thanks to the sun's strange behavior exists here in different proportions. A year is one long diurnal cycle of cold night and blistering light day. The celestial clock turns rather majestically when you live right underneath the pendulum.

Presumably that figure on the steps was thinking of nothing and allowing time to trickle straight through. David was forced to think about different things, making funeral orations over himself and summoning up an image of cold beer, so as not to make any involuntary movement. Or quite simply leap out and say, "Well, here I am. Can you really shoot when you see the infinite blue of my eyes?"

The sun was sailing in the total lack of wind. David felt he was in a time vacuum but found that the shadows were changing and lengthening. Soon the sun would be above that turf roof, he thought, just to have something to think about. But at that moment, the thought struck him like a sandbag on the back of his head and he felt like Scheele at the moment he discovered oxygen.

This was when the terror arrived. It did not creep up on him or cautiously whisper a hint of the outcome into his ear. It came like a brass band and exploded with sound effects in his ears and flashing pictures in front of his eyes. He saw it all with a clarity he had never experienced before. In yet another half an hour, the sun would creep over the barn opening and slowly begin to play on planking and lumber. First it would take his left hand and then grope its way up his body. It was only a minor matter of time now before he would be dazzlingly exposed in his hiding place.

He spent the time before the first rays of the sun poked at the gray timbers thinking about absolutely nothing. Then he started considering ways out, but there was none. Not unless that figure out there would get up and leave. And there wasn't much chance of that.

He started cautiously twitching the muscles of his legs without moving, to reduce the numbness. But the obstinate prickling as his blood started circulating was worse than the lack of sensation. He almost cried with irritation. Forty-five minutes after his discovery of the merciless movement of the sun, though without having the slightest idea of the time, he dipped his fingers in sunlight.

Ironically he enjoyed the warmth. It felt like the caressing touch of an impersonally friendly person. He started staring through the cracks at the face on the steps, and those darting eyes that never stopped moving between the buildings. David never noticed the sun taking possession of his hand and starting to climb up his arm. He was suddenly totally fascinated by a phenomenon on the face of the person waiting for him out there. A dazzling reflection of the sun was trembling like a bright spot on the sweaty forehead.

David was no longer as still as he ought to have been, though he failed to notice it. He was far too intent on staring at that yellowish-white reflection dancing from the forehead to the shoulder. There it stopped for a moment, then moved up to the throat, indecorously playful in a situation where David could not discern the slightest humorous element. For a moment it flashed away to the window alongside—a bold leap, and it had to be assumed that it bounced back off the old man's face in there. It was quickly out again and stood trembling and crestfallen at its starting position on that forehead.

David had now leaned forward, soundlessly and without noticing. He could no longer feel the prickling in his leg. He could feel nothing at all. The moment he turned his arm a little, the reflection moved down into the eye.

It all occurred in time that was not measurable. The eye was dazzled by the reflection—a widening and astonished look. Suddenly, David understood. His arm jerked and the reflection had gone from the eye. He could see that the reflection came from the mirror-bright back of his wristwatch. It was circular like a clock face and absolutely synchronized with his movements. The very next moment he saw how circular the mouth of the rifle barrel was.

He thought it was going to go off immediately, but the mouth of the barrel was seeking uncertainly for him. No more of him was visible than the flashing watch circle. David never knew whether it was intentional or not, but the reflection maneuvered itself up to the eye again. Once it was there, it was not difficult to keep it going, with small arm movements, between the two eyes in a face that kept trying to avoid the flash in order to be able to look down the gun sight.

He would not have been able to go on for long. But a voice suddenly sliced through the silence of this sun-heated oven.

"Run! *Täällä, senkin idootti* [Over here, you idiot]!"

The shot went off and he ran. He knew at once it was not a good one. It splintered the boards on his right, and he threw himself to the left out of the barn and saw the rifle barrel turn in the other direction. Somewhere out of the corner of his eye, he saw a figure waving his arms about—a target right in the middle of the cattle track. Then he fell flat on his face in the dry, spiky grass and his legs collapsed numbly beneath him. The end, he thought. My back.

The second shot rang out and his eardrums seemed to rip like sailcloth. He lay flat for a long time, listening to the emptiness that followed. He had no idea what he would see on the cattle track and he didn't much care by the time he managed to gather his legs under him and go forward.

"You're alive?"

"Aye."

The buzz of flies had not stopped. The sun continued to creep over the barn wall.

"I thought you were dead, sitting there in the cabin."

"Ei [No]. I was just waiting."

Edvin pressed his leather cap more firmly down over his forehead and started fumbling with his snuff. For some reason, he was looking embarrassed.

"Where . . . ?" asked David, his lips dry, and the old man nodded over toward the other side of the barn.

"You might've been shot when you jumped out of the cottage."

"Aye. I saw your watch flashing in the sun."

"I . . . I would never have done that for you," said David, the words coming in a rush.

"No. Why should you?" The old man shook briefly with inner laughter.

They walked through the long grass around the barn. Henrik Vuori was lying on his back with the gun in his arms. David couldn't see where he had been hit, but there was blood running out of the corner of his mouth.

"I managed to get around the corner," said Edvin, unexpectedly brightly. "I jumped out as he came along. Straight into his arms. He was holding the gun himself when it went off and we hugged each other. Look at him—my friend. This morning he cornered me in the kitchen and said that I wasn't to say anything about him helping me bury Aili. "I'm Swedish," he said, "so they'll go harder on me if I was involved in such a thing. It's not exactly natural for me," he—my friend—said. Now let's go back to Rakisjokk."

"We can't very well leave him lying there."

"Oh, yes, we can."

He went over to the porch steps and examined his water bottle.

"We'll have to manage without. What did you come here for?"

"I was going to ask you who helped you with her . . . last summer. It occurred to me you weren't alone on it."

"No, it was his idea. But he knew perfectly well someone would come and ask in the end. Aye, he was the one to help me. And Henrik Vuori was the one who so kindly told me that Matti was the father of the child Aili was expecting."

"But he wasn't?"

"*Ei.* It was Henrik himself. He was all set to marry that Marta woman plus her inheritance from her father, see. Aili went off the same day. I don't believe he ever took his hand to Aili, though he probably said something to her. But he didn't dare let it come out what had happened to her, for then that father's inheritance would probably have gone back home to Kuivakangas again. So he thought up all that about Matti. Now I understand why Aili never looked at Matti."

"How did you get away from him when he came in among the houses?"

"I saw the barrel of his rifle and his eyes around the corner of the cottage, and I don't know what got into him. Something quite peculiar, it was. *"Mitä sinä sitten tahdot?"* I said, in sheer surprise."

"What's that mean?"

"What do you want?" For a moment I thought he was going to give me the gun. Then I started running. I knocked over the water bottle and threw myself in between the houses. I hid in this one here. I thought I could wait."

Suddenly Edvin snapped his mouth shut as if he thought his ration of words had been used up for the next fourteen months, and he started walking ahead of David with calm, soft steps. They had entered the forest.

The big policeman was striding to and fro in front of the house, the dog watching him with watery eyes. Torsson was scratching at his stubble and mumbling to himself as if trying to learn a part.

"Torsson!" David shouted, breathless after the march from Poropirtti.

"Be quiet for a moment."

David stopped, his arms hanging down. "Well, now, bloody hell, to put it bluntly," he said, sinking down on the bottom step.

"Now then," said Torsson in a milder voice, with a glance up toward the Jerfs' cottage, where the gold-braided one's profile could be seen in the window. "It's just that it's so difficult, you see. We're going back now. I don't know what to do. I have to speak to him. But what shall I say?" He shook himself and then noticed David again. "What did you want?"

"Nothing," said David firmly. "Absolutely nothing. Let's save it up for Christmas."

Torsson gave him a strange look. "The state of you," he said mildly. "Oh, well."

He took David by the arm and drew him away a bit toward the brewhouse, his eyes all the time on the window of the cottage. But they could see nothing behind the blue checked curtains.

"I thought I must speak to him, anyhow. Now that I know who he is. But I don't know how to put it. I haven't got much to go on. But you probably realized yourself that it must have been one of the people who didn't play mah-jongg?"

"No," said David patiently. "I didn't."

"You see, one of the mah-jongg players would have known that a tile was missing in that hand that got swept onto the floor. That was the green dragon I found. A mah-jongg player would have looked for it. It wasn't hard to find. But that doesn't tell us anything, does it?"

"No, not much. Whatever it is you want to have told."

"But as soon as Marta came along with that rope story, then I understood. It was very clever of him to let her go on and on about it. He really was going to tell us. It was just that he happened to see that I unlocked the door. Then he changed his mind. The room had been locked all the time. So it was all a lie. But he didn't know Marta came back and told us. She couldn't restrain herself."

"But I can," said David, with emphasis on every syllable.

"You're *yawning?* Are you crazy?"

"I'm just desperately tired, totally flaked out."

"It all looked so satisfactory," Torsson went on, "that he'd spent the hours after the party when Matti died with his wife in the marital bed. Even though Marta would surely have been able to cook up some story to protect him, she wouldn't have done in this case, I don't think — when he'd brought misfortune on another woman. However, it wasn't needed. They say he has to sleep on the kitchen bench when he's been drinking. So she never noticed when he came home."

"Really."

"You might at least take some interest. This is about your friend Matti. He was just as you thought, a nice lad. So all that's left now is what I'm going to say to the man."

"You needn't talk to Henrik Vuori. You can't. He's lying dead in Poropirtti."

"What did you say?"

Torsson slowly swung around and grabbed David's arms, pinning them to his sides and shaking him back and forth so that David hung like a puppet in his great fists. Torsson was babbling like a lunatic.

"Is that true? What's Poropirtti? Why didn't you say something? Are you out of your mind?"

"Yes, why didn't I say anything?" David mumbled. "Unforgivable of me."

The police boat didn't get away from Rakisjokk until the second day. It was a clear, chilly morning, the mountain ridge beyond the village outlined against clear sky as seen from out on the lake. Reluctantly, the pale green seaweed had let go of the propeller and allowed the boat to disturb the icy morning reflection of cloudberry clumps in the water on the shore. Torsson stood in the bow watching Rakisjokk being reduced to a blur below the mountain. When the schoolhouse disappeared, he was about to turn around but was stopped by a reflection from the sun in the far distance. It flashed, hesitantly at first and then more and more clearly. As far out as halfway to Orjas, the lightning flash from Rakisjokk followed him. All he could see was an impassive mountain with no cloud cap against the cold of space, and down at its foot this living flash playfully leaping in the blue-green mist along the shore, refusing to leave him until the boat changed its course.

In Rakisjokk, Per-Anders Jerf went up on the hill above his house and stood looking at David.

"Have you dragged out the washstand mirror?" he inquired on a note of curiosity.

"Yes," replied David, "I thought I'd dazzle Torsson a little."

He was holding the mirror upright in his arms and

maneuvering it carefully to the right and left, capturing the sun in the glass.

Per-Anders looked out over the lake. "So you'll be staying awhile, will you?"

"Aye."

About the Author

Kerstin Ekman is one of Sweden's most prominent novelists. She was born in 1933 in Risinge, a small village in the middle of Sweden. She has written seventeen novels which have been widely published in other Scandinavian languages, German, Finnish, Dutch, and French, and have won numerous prizes and awards. Her most recent novel, *Blackwater,* has been awarded the Swedish Crime Academy's Award for the best crime novel, the August Prize, and the Nordic Council's Literary Prize. She became a member of the Swedish Academy of Arts and Letters in 1978 but resigned in 1989 when the academy did not make a statement that she could approve of about the Rushdie case. She lives in Valsjöbyn, a small village in the north of Sweden.